A THREAD OF MADNESS

BLYTHE BAKER

Copyright © 2020 by Blythe Baker

All rights reserved.

No part of this book may be reproduced in any form or by any electronic or mechanical means, including information storage and retrieval systems, without written permission from the author, except for the use of brief quotations in a book review.

❀ Created with Vellum

DESCRIPTION

A sudden death uncovers a string of secrets in a small village...

When seamstresses Iris and Lily Dickinson are accidental witnesses to a murder, the spinster sisters resolve to keep themselves – and their pristine reputations – a discreet distance away from the sordid business. But the unexpected discovery that the killer might be in their very midst soon changes everything, sparking an urgent desperation to ferret out his identity.

While assisting the local constable in his investigation, Iris stumbles across a family mystery of her own, a buried secret that calls into question everything she thinks she knows about her sister. With Iris's once-blind faith in Lily shaken, can the sisters unite long enough to escape the schemes of a dangerous lunatic?

1

Death had always been a part of my life, hulking like a shadow over me, casting its long reach across my past to stretch into my future. It claimed those I loved, it shrouded murky memories in secrecy, and a time would come when it would stretch out its sharp claws to drag me toward the abyss, as well.

But that did not mean I was always aware of danger. Indeed, sometimes I scarcely noticed its presence as it flitted like a dark cloud at the edge of my vision. In the simple life I lived in the quiet little Yorkshire town of Grangehurst, it was all too easy not to look deeper than the sunny surface, not to see the dark shapes that moved beneath the ripples of my calm existence...

The days seemed to meander when I was a child, as I never cared much for the difference between them.

It was a happy childhood, shared with my dear sister, nearly ten years my elder. Even after our parents, vague figures whom I could recall little of, passed away while I was young, life changed very little. My sister and I simply moved across town to live with an aunt and uncle.

When the generosity of our relatives ran dry, my sister took up a needle and thread to support us both. That choice would lead us down the path where we would find ourselves on one particular autumn afternoon many years later...

I BLINKED in the sunlight streaming in through the shop windows. Reining in my wondering thoughts, I realized that I was neglecting a customer.

"Good afternoon, Mrs. Minford," I said with a smile as I caught sight of the short woman with hunched shoulders. "How are you doing this fine day?"

Mrs. Minford looked up at me, squinting as she always did, her wrinkled face splitting into a smile to match my own. "Ah, Miss Iris, dear. Quite well, quite well, all things considered. I managed to wrangle those pesky moles from my yard this week. Well, Mr. Perkins was able to. I simply watched."

I laughed as I folded the beautiful blue linen that reminded me of the night sky in the middle of winter, the bolt it was to be rolled into lying beside me on the counter I stood behind.

"Well, I'm pleased to hear it. Perhaps you should supervise our own mole extraction. Poor Lily is nearly at her wits end about her begonias; the little imps nearly destroyed them this past summer."

"What was that, Iris?"

I glanced over my shoulder to the back of the small shop.

A slim woman knelt behind a long, ivory, satin train of a gown, a needle pinched tightly between her thumb and forefinger as she looked up at me.

Taller than I was by nearly a head, my sister Lily was the exact opposite of me in many ways. Where her hair was nearly as dark as a bottle of ink, mine could be more closely compared to a field of wheat at the time of harvest. Her eyes, stern and grey, were like the clouds in the dead of winter, whereas my eyes were as blue as the summer skies.

"Oh, it's nothing, sister," I said. "Mrs. Minford was commenting on the moles in her garden, and I told her how they had disturbed your garden so terribly just this last – "

"I am rather busy at the moment to be worrying about moles," Lily said, her dark eyebrows knitting together. "Mrs. Minford, you must excuse my sister for her idle chatter. I'm certain she will be happy to help you with whatever it is you need."

She turned away from me then, her attention back to the needle that she worked deftly along the hem of the dress.

The young woman wearing the dress glanced over

her shoulder to see precisely what it was that Lily was adding to the train, but said nothing as Lily continued to work.

I turned back to Mrs. Minford with an apologetic smile. "I'm afraid my sister is rather distracted at the moment," I said. "You know how she is when she becomes focused."

Mrs. Minford nodded knowingly as she squinted back toward the corner of the room where Lily worked. "Oh, indeed I do," she said.

"Was there something I could help you with?" I asked, setting the navy linen aside, clearing the space between us.

Mrs. Minford reached into the bag that she had carried inside with her, and pulled out three small embroidery hoops, setting them down before me.

I gasped, lifting the first one I saw. It was an intricate design of a white rose on a background of green silk.

"Mrs. Minford, this is extraordinary," I said, examining the hoop from all angles. "I am truly having difficulty not believing it to be a real flower that you have simply stitched onto the fabric itself!"

Mrs. Minford gave me a shy smile. "Oh, you are too kind," she said. "I am pleased that you like them."

"Like them?" I asked. "I am astonished, as I always am, by your immaculate needlepoint."

Mrs. Minford bowed her head humbly. "Well...you are sweet, Miss Iris."

I looked at the other two; a small bouquet of bluebells upon a white silk backdrop, and a third with a simple filigree design upon a grey linen, meant to be stitched into the hem of a handkerchief.

"And how are you doing with your needlepoint?" she asked. "Having any time to practice?"

My eyes darted down to the hoops in my hands once again. "Oh, yes, I have practiced when I have the chance, of course. Lately, however, we have had so many orders that I've had little time. Mrs. Newman was in just a week ago, and ordered new dresses for each of her daughters for Christmas; apparently, they are going to Oxford to stay with her uncle, and she wanted to purchase something nice for them to wear. And then we must not forget Mr. Kurt coming in, asking for a new set of gloves for his wife, but he asked specifically for a type of silk that we had no choice but to order from out of the country...And as you saw, Lily has been working hard on Miss Baldwin's wedding dress, which she will be needing in just over a fortnight – "

Mrs. Minford, squinting up at me, chuckled. "It was not my intention to make you uneasy, dear girl," she said.

I frowned at her. "I am sorry. I do promise to pick it up again as soon as I am able."

Mrs. Minford shrugged her shoulders. "I am always happy to teach. Of course, I won't be around forever. Knowing that you and your sister can continue this wonderful business of yours makes it more than worth the effort to teach you something small like this."

"Small?" I asked, gesturing to the intricate hoops. "This is no small matter."

"It is when compared to the lovely garments that you both make," Mrs. Minford said with a nod. "Ever since you and your sister opened this shop, the town has been much better off for it." She leaned forward. "And so much more handsomely dressed."

I smiled. "You are far too kind."

Mrs. Minford regarded me for a long moment. "You know, I am surprised that some handsome young man has not come along and married you," she said, shaking her head. "You are such a sweet girl, and to be your age and unmarried…"

I blushed, turning to pick up the tin where we tucked away some extra money. "Oh, I imagine it's because I am not much of a traveler," I said. "I suppose if I had gone to London to visit my cousins more, perhaps I would have attended more of those elegant parties and balls that they so love."

"Perhaps," Mrs. Minford said.

I passed the payment across to her, smiling, though my cheeks were still quite warm. "Here, this is for the needlepoint," I said. "Thank you once again. These will be lovely on the projects we have chosen them for."

Mrs. Minford gazed down at the money for a few moments before meeting my gaze once again. The look on her face told me that she considered saying something else to me, but decided against it. So she smiled instead. "Thank you," she said. "And I look forward to seeing the finished items. Let me know if you need anything else from me, I am always happy to help with whatever it is you might need."

She tipped her head to me. "Have a good day, Miss Iris," she said, and then leaned to look past me, squinting her eyes. "And you have a good day as well, Miss Lily," she said.

Lily lifted a hand and waved without taking her eyes from the dress, a pencil clamped tightly between her teeth.

"See you soon," I said as Mrs. Minford turned and wandered back toward the door.

When she pulled it open, brilliant October sunshine washed in over the threshold. As she stepped outside, I heard the hustle and bustle of the small town in the late afternoon, the bark of our neighbor's dog George the third, and the carrying on of children on their way home from the schoolhouse.

I wandered through the tables laden with cloth and examples of some of the latest fashions adorned on a variety of mannequins that Lily had painstakingly constructed herself, making my way toward the window that looked out onto the street.

The day was beautiful for the middle of autumn. The trees peeked out behind the buildings across Front Street, the main street, which was the only road that saw any sort of traffic in all of Grangehurst. The buildings were all made of the same weathered stone that had survived many, many years of the harsh Yorkshire winters, with tall chimneys with tendrils of smoke that would caress the cloudy skies in the cold days that were soon to come.

Our shop, at the end of a row of other homes and shops, was smaller than the rest, but right in the center of town. Most people passed by it as they went about their days, and the local ladies were generally delighted that we had taken up the charge of bringing in a place of fashion so nearby.

I peered outside into the street, seeing a few people passing by. I recognized one as Reverend Michaels, whose church down the street was nestled on top of the hill. He was walking with old Doctor Webb, the two of them with their heads together, speaking of some philosophical matters, no doubt. I also noticed Mrs. Clark, the baker's wife. A pretty woman with hair like the depths of a lively flame, she had the shape of a woman who had given birth to more children than most, but had the smile of one who would have it no other way. I wondered if she carried any of her husband's famous mince pies in that basket she wore in the crook of her arm.

Another gentleman, rather easy to distinguish from other townsfolk, crossed the street up nearer to the pub at the intersection of Front Street and River Road. A tall man, with broad shoulders, narrow hips, and the countenance of one who had spent nearly his entire life in the military. Captain Seymour was an older resident recently returned, who seemed to have all the local ladies abuzz with infatuations and flirtations. Lily admitted he was handsome enough, but he must have easily been twenty years her elder. Even still, it was the first time that I could recall my sister admitting to finding someone even the least bit attractive.

Further along the street, I knew the landscape dropped off into a gorge, with the river Bernes running through it. As one passed over the bridge that crossed it, the ancient aqueducts could be seen further up the river, grounding this little town in a history as deep and wide as the country herself.

"Iris, if you are quite done examining the windows, could you please come and lend me your assistance?" Lily asked from the back of the shop.

"Coming," I said, turning away from the window and making my way back to where she stood with the bride-to-be.

"Miss Baldwin, you look stunning," I said as I approached the three mirrors we had erected in the corner, all three at an angle so the customer would be able to see herself nearly all the way around.

The young woman, about a decade younger than I was, with blushing cheeks and full lips, stared up at me, wonder in her eyes. "It's more beautiful than anything I could have imagined," she said, her gaze unable to wander far from the satin and silk for more than a few moments time. "I knew white gowns had become quite fashionable in London ever since the Queen wore one for her wedding, but I never imagined I would wear such a lovely gown myself…"

Lily clicked her tongue in annoyance. "If you could please stand still, Miss Baldwin, this adjustment would be much easier," she said. "And your dress is ivory, not white."

The color rose in Miss Baldwin's face. "My apologies," she said, lowering her head like a chastised pup.

"Oh, cheer up," I said. "Lily's needlework is the best in the north, and I assure you, she will not let you part with the dress until she considers it perfect, which means it certainly will be."

Lily glanced up at me, a small spool of ivory thread clamped between her lips. She arched an eyebrow.

"Let me see," I said, stepping behind the bride, checking to see what it was that Lily was doing. "Ah, yes. The button work in the back is exquisite, a fine detail in and of itself. Some ladies have ruffles, others bows…but Lily and I believe that these sorts of buttons make for a much more feminine line. See how it doesn't bunch the fabric here beneath the arms? How the sleeves fall so nicely?"

I placed my pointer finger gently against the inside of her waist, and then up on her arm.

"It's all intentional, of course, to bring out the very best of your physique," Lily said, pulling the thread from her mouth and deftly threading yet another needle with it. "What is the point of a dress, if not to make one as pleasing to the eye as possible?"

I rolled my eyes upwards, allowing a small laugh. "Indeed, sister, but it is also meant to make the wearer feel pleased with herself. And does it make you happy, Miss Baldwin?"

"Oh, good heavens, yes," Miss Baldwin said with an

eager nod. "I am certain I shall be the happiest bride there ever was."

It took some coaxing, but I finally convinced Lily to be satisfied with the needlework near the buttons, and we helped Miss Baldwin change back into a simple, green dress that made the color of her eyes stand out.

She thanked us profusely, promising to be back within the next three or four days to collect the garment before the wedding at the end of the month.

I waved as she hurried from the door, the smile on her face so large it was contagious. "Goodbye!" she said, the joy flowing from her in waves.

I caught Lily looking at me as Miss Baldwin closed the door behind herself, hurrying out into the street, the sunlight bathing her face as she passed.

"What is it?" I asked.

Lily sighed, shaking her head. "I got caught up again, didn't I?"

She turned around and walked back to the trio of mirrors, stooping to collect her scissors, her pin cushion, and the extra satin she had hemmed away from the train. "I do this every time we have a bride come through," she said. "I somehow leave everything else to you and become far too absorbed in the task at hand to realize that half the day has passed."

"It's quite all right," I said. "I took Mrs. Collier's order, and made the adjustments for Mrs. Newman, who wants now to have a dress made for her niece as an early Christmas present."

"The same as the others?" Lily asked, somewhat heavily.

I nodded. "The very same."

Lily sighed, standing up straight once again. "Very well," she said. "Is that something you can manage? I must take on Mr. Kurt's order, as he hoped to collect the gloves by Friday."

"Yes, of course," I said. My sister was the better with the details of the two of us, so it made sense that I left the more intricate tasks to her.

Lily turned to look at the mannequin where the dress was hanging, beautiful in the warm afternoon light.

"I suppose you wish you could have worn a dress like this…" she said, her voice uncharacteristically soft.

Her words caught me off guard. "Yes, well…I imagine every young woman hopes to wear a wedding gown someday, doesn't she?"

Lily lifted an eyebrow. "Perhaps not *every* young woman," she said, returning to her usual brisk self.

I do wonder why Lily never sought to marry…as intelligent and capable as she is in all that she does, I am surprised she was never approached. Or perhaps she was, and she simply has never shared that with me.

She was nine years older than I, almost ten…I imagined there was a great deal about her life that she had never shared with me.

There is always the possibility that life simply passed her by…time moves so quickly, and she has worked tirelessly these last ten or fifteen years in order to build a business for herself...for us, really... everything we have is because of the sweat of my sister's brow.

I walked over to Lily and laid a hand on her arm.

She turned, pulling her gaze from the wedding dress. "What is it?" she asked.

"I just want you to know how grateful I am," I said. "For all you have done for me. For us."

Lily shifted uncomfortably beneath my touch, stepping away from it and stooping to pick up the bolt of fabric she had used to measure the slip for the wedding dress. "It is the result of hard work from both of us," she said. "You have helped make this whole endeavor possible."

She glanced at the clock on the wall, the minute hand hovering just past the eleven. "Well...I don't imagine we will be receiving any more customers today. Why don't we lock up and retire for the evening?"

The sun outside had begun to dip down behind the tree line across the street to the west. "Very well," I said.

I tucked the spools of thread into the drawers where they belonged while Lily placed the bolts of fabric back into their designated slots along the wall where we had easy access to them. Then, together, we turned toward the doors leading up to our rooms above the store.

Another day come, another day gone. I was already looking forward to what I was sure would be a quiet, uneventful evening.

"Iris, would you care for sugar in your tea this evening?" Lily asked.

I looked up from my spot beside the fireplace. It was along the wall in our small sitting room, which was just off the kitchen and the single bedroom that we shared.

It was a comfortable space for two, though it made entertaining guests difficult at times. Our small table, which stood in a nook beside the window, had only four, simple wooden chairs wrapped around it, a gift from the carpenter in town, who was a friend of our aunt and uncle. A short sofa stood before the fire, with two armchairs that Lily and I had reupholstered ourselves, flanking it on either side. Tall bookshelves stood behind each chair, and a round, well-worn rug was sprawled out beneath the tightly packed furniture.

I set the needlepoint I had begun to work on again that evening down on the table beside me, looking about toward the kitchen, where the bright, warm glow of the candles used inside spilled out. "I will have some sugar, please," I said.

I heard the *tink* of a spoon against the teacups, and a moment later, she appeared with a silver tray in her hands.

She set it down on the low table in front of the sofa, where she gingerly sat. "Here you are," she said, passing my cup to me.

It was a favorite of mine, simple with gold and pink

designs of roses painted onto the china. I sipped it tentatively; it was still overly warm.

I wrinkled my nose. *Not enough sugar again...*

Lily set her tea down, glancing at the small hoop I'd set down on the table. "Picking up your needlepoint once more, I see," she said, arching her brow. "May I?"

I nodded, still attempting to sip from my own cup.

She examined the simple linen, both front and back, and nodded her head. "These peonies are quite good," she said.

I frowned. "They aren't meant to be peonies," I said, lowering my cup, staring at the back of my design with growing frustration. "It's meant to be a begonia. As I know they are your favorite."

Lily smiled, setting the hoop down upon the table. "To be perfectly fair, they are similar in appearance," she said. "I see it now. You have done quite well."

"You do not have to patronize me," I said, picking up the hoop, frowning at it. "I suppose I am rather glad that Mrs. Minford did not see this...especially not with the lovely designs that she brought in with her today."

"I saw them," Lily said. "They were exquisite. I trust you paid her for them?"

I nodded. "I would not forget something that important again," I said. "Certainly not."

Lily nodded. "Very good. And I saw you speaking with Mrs. Newman?"

"Oh, yes," I said, sipping the tea once more. *Still not sweet enough...* "She was particularly excited about something today. Apparently, there was quite the commotion in the market. Captain Seymour approached one of the stalls asking for seeds. It seems he wanted sunflower seeds in particular. He was told that sunflower seeds were not in season, and he seemed terribly disappointed. When asked what he wanted them for, he responded that they were for his parrot!"

"Parrot?" Lily asked, furrowing her dark eyebrows. "The man owns a parrot?"

"It seems so, yes," I said. "A rather strange choice, wouldn't you say?"

"He spent how many years in India?" Lily asked. "I suppose one would pick up some rather...unfortunate habits living in another country."

I smiled at her. "Just because you wouldn't want such an unusual pet doesn't mean that it's wrong."

"Look at the sort of commotion it caused, though," Lily said. "No one could believe that any sane man would own a parrot. It's bizarre. He draws the wrong sort of attention to himself, wouldn't you say?"

"It's also rather exciting, isn't it?" I asked. "To have such an exotic creature in one's home would be an adventure, I think."

"Why am I not surprised you would say so?" Lily asked, sipping her tea.

After a moment's silence, she nudged a box toward me, a small item I hadn't noticed on the table before. "Here," she said. "I thought you might enjoy these."

My eyes widened as I looked at the small package. I

took it, untied the ribbon with ginger fingers, and opened it.

It was filled with beautiful, individually wrapped chocolates, each with an imprint of the local confectioner's own design, painted in white chocolate dyed red.

"Oh, Lily, these are lovely," I said. "They must have been an expense!"

She gave one of her rare smiles. "Remember when I was at the post office most of the afternoon last week? I may have fibbed a bit. I went in to look at something for you for Christmas this year, and I ended up being asked to help Mrs. Clark with some of their curtains that had been ripped by her youngest attempting to climb up them. After I was finished, she offered me these, and I happily accepted, knowing you would enjoy them."

I picked one out of the box and unwrapped it from the crinkling, sheer wrapper.

The smell of the rich, buttery chocolate greeted me at once, making my mouth water.

My eyes closed as I took a bite and savored the warm, rich flavor. "They're wonderful. Sweet, soft, and the center reminds me of the texture of clotted cream." I held out the rest of the small square. "Here, you should try it too."

Lily shook her head. "No, those are for you," she said, leaving her seat and walking back to the kitchen. "You know I don't care for sweets."

I settled back into my chair with my chocolates,

contently picking up a novel I had been reading earlier.

I cannot imagine a more relaxing evening. Hot tea by the fire, with chocolates and a good story...

Lily made us a fresh pot of tea and brought it back into the sitting room a short time later; I had read nearly a full chapter and eaten two more squares of chocolate by that point.

"Now, tomorrow, I should like to finish the veil for Miss Baldwin's dress," Lily said. "I would like you to go down to the haberdashery and pick up some of that ivory ribbon that we have been – "

A bark or some such sound echoed outside in the street.

Lily and I looked at one another. It sounded different from the barks that belonged to our neighbor's dog.

"What on earth could that have been?" Lily asked, rising from her seat and making her way to the window along the wall.

I set down my novel and joined her at the window.

From our little shop, we had a decent view of the street, both upward and back. The few streetlamps that were in place along the road had been lit, glowing warmly in the darkness, casting pools of brightness up and down the length of the avenue.

The pub at the end of the street seemed as busy as it typically was in the evenings, with every window bright, and the front doors thrown open. I was very nearly certain that I could hear music streaming out, likely Mr. Franklin, who played the violin better than any person I had ever known.

A few men gathered around the front of the pub, but closer to our home, where the street was empty, a shape wandered in a not so straight line.

Another bark bounced off the brick buildings, and I realized it was coming from him.

"Oh, it's only Mr. Morton..." Lily said in a tone of disgust. "Why am I not surprised that he is out making such a racket?"

I watched him stumble down the street, nearly tripping over his own boots. He let out a booming laugh that was even louder than his barking shout had been just moments before.

Lily turned away and went back to the sofa, where she picked up her tea.

"It's rather sad," I said. "To see him reduced to such a state."

"What, as the town drunkard?" Lily asked. "He may not have chosen the circumstances in his life, but he certainly did have the choice not to behave the way he does. He could have made something else of himself. Instead, he wastes his money down at the pub, drowning his problems at the bottom of a tankard."

I frowned down at the man. I remembered him from when I was a child. "Lily, do you remember when he owned that beautiful toy shop?" I asked. "Where he made those rocking horses with the red ribbons tied around their necks?"

Lily let out a soft "Hmph," and continued to sip her tea.

I looked back out the window, watching him come closer and closer to the shop, likely heading back to his house, which was down past the intersection, and off down the south roads to a small cottage at the edge of town.

"Such a long way to walk at such an hour…" I mumbled.

A dark shape appeared in the pool of light, like a silhouette of ink, making a dash for Mr. Morton's back.

He stepped from the pool of light into the patches of shadows between the streetlamps, and the inky shape disappeared as well.

I blinked, shaking my head. *What did I just see?*

Mr. Morton's voice emerged from the shadows, singing loudly, and rather offkey, a sea shanty that he seemed to only know half the words to.

"Oh, good heavens…" Lily said. "I have half a mind to shout out the window and tell him off."

"He's not harming anyone," I said, my eyes glued to the next pool of light, waiting for him to reappear.

"He's disturbing the peace," Lily said in a sharp tone.

I watched him step into the pool of light, still singing – and the shadow that followed appeared right behind him.

"What is that?" I asked, leaning forward. "Lily, there is something following Mr. Morton – "

The shadow moved like a shot, and collided with Mr. Morton's back.

Mr. Morton stopped in his tracks, the words to his sea shanty dying in his throat.

"Oh, no!" I exclaimed.

Mr. Morton crumpled to the ground, and the shadow dashed away from the pools of light, disappearing.

2

My heart hammered in my chest as I stared out at the motionless figure of Mr. Morton, lying in the middle of the street. A ringing in my ears grew louder the longer I looked, unable to tear my gaze away.

That shadow...what was it? Who was it?

I blinked a few times, rubbing my eyes with the backs of my hands.

He couldn't have been...no, that's utterly preposterous.

Was it, though? Was it entirely impossible to think that he might have been – could have been –

But why was that my first thought?

Killed.

An icy chill ran from the base of my neck all the way down my back.

As I looked down at him, I knew something was wrong. A man did not simply collapse the way he had...and not to mention the bizarre shadow that had appeared behind him. Were my eyes playing tricks on me?

I searched the streets, my heart in my throat. Where had that shadow gotten to?

I knew perfectly well that an ordinary *shadow* couldn't hurt someone, so it had to have been some*one* obscured by the night.

But he cannot be dead...surely not. Surely, I am seeing things...I must be tired. There is a perfectly reasonable explanation. Mr. Morton is a heavy drinker, and it is not uncommon for people who have had a great deal to drink to collapse like that in a stupor. Isn't that a far more sensible explanation to what has occurred? Or am I simply going mad?

I bit down on the end of my thumb, my mind racing. My eyes fixed on the man in the middle of the street, each passing second an agony as I willed him to rise, to get up, to dust himself off with a laugh and carry on his way.

"What's the matter?" Lily asked.

I looked around and found my sister staring at me, her eyes narrowed. "You look as if you've seen a ghost," she said sternly, though I detected a note of worry in her voice.

"It's Mr. Morton," I said, pointing to the window. "He – he won't get up, and I – "

Lily let out a sigh and rose from the sofa, coming over to stand beside me at the window once more. "What are you seeing?" she asked, leaning down and peering outside.

"He fell down," I said, my mouth suddenly dry. "I'm not certain what happened. One moment he was perfectly fine, and the next – "

Lily's cross expression quickly changed to one of alarm. "Good heavens, he's collapsed," she said.

It seemed that we were not the only ones to have noticed. Some of the men gathered outside the pub had made their way down the street, likely having seen Mr. Morton fall to the ground. They knelt beside him, obscuring him from our sight.

Lily sighed once again. "We might as well see what's happened," she said. "I certainly do not wish to hear Mrs. Minford's version of this come morning. She will have heard it from someone, who will have likely told her husband, who will then share it with her, and you know that she will do her best to exaggerate every detail."

She turned and marched to the door.

I glanced out the window once more. My heart, like that of a rabbit attempting to flee a hawk, thundered inside my aching chest. I rose from the windowsill and hurried to fetch my shawl. Throwing it around my shoulders, I quickly followed after my sister.

We stepped out into the dark, chilled street. The sun's absence left the air bitter, reminding us that winter was not far behind.

Lily, already several steps ahead of me, walked fearlessly toward Mr. Morton, her breath visible in the night air.

I hurried to catch up with her, but realized she was

not going to make it very far when she was stopped by a familiar figure.

The town's face of the law, Constable Brown. A kind man, even if a bit dim on occasion, he was skilled enough when it came to weeding out the local wrongdoers and troublemakers.

Some might have found him handsome, with his tall, lean build, but I was never able to see past the sizable gap between his front teeth, nor the way that he seemed to incessantly run his fingers through his sandy beard when he spoke.

"Wait just one moment, Miss Dickinson," he said, frowning beneath his constabulary hat, and stepping in front of my sister. "This here is a troubling scene, and I would not like you or your sister to distress yourselves with it."

"Thank you for your thoughtfulness, Constable, but I am a grown woman, and am quite certain I am able to handle the truth of whatever has happened here," Lily said in a curt tone. "We saw the man collapse and simply wish to know..."

She found herself speaking to the Constable's back, however, as he was already hurrying off to where a group had gathered around the fallen man.

An elderly gentleman with a white mustache approached us. It seemed our neighbor, Mr. Crawford, had overheard the brief exchange.

"I am sure the Constable meant nothing by it, Miss Dickinson, but there seems to be some real trouble brewing here, and I imagine we citizens will have to keep our distance," he said kindly.

I reached my sister's side and stared nervously past Mr. Crawford to where the Constable and three men from the pub were kneeling down beside Mr. Morton, hiding him from us. "What's happened?"

"Apparently, we aren't to know," Lily said. "We noticed he had collapsed from the window in our home, and wished to come and see if the poor man was all right."

Mr. Crawford, concern written across his face, looked back over his shoulder. "It seems no one is sure," he said. "I only just arrived but I heard the doctor has been sent for. The Constable was fetched by Mr. Parcel, over there."

Mr. Parcel was indeed there, his balding head giving him away as he knelt beside the still body of Mr. Morton.

As Mr. Crawford excused himself and wandered away, Lily glanced over her shoulder. "It appears we aren't the only ones curious about what happened…"

I followed her gaze, finding a few others gathered further down the street. Another neighbor, Miss Violet, stood just outside her door, holding tight to the collar of her dog, who sniffed the air eagerly, tugging against his mistress's grasp. Mrs. Minford, at the house on the corner of the far intersection further up the road, could be seen with her nightcap, standing behind her husband, who did not seem too keen to let her out to investigate, his one hand outstretched to protect her, the other holding a lantern aloft.

"Gawking, as she usually is…" Lily murmured, turning away.

"What we are doing isn't much better," I said.

"I simply want to know the truth," Lily said. "I will not have rumors permeating our shop for the rest of the week. You know as well as I do that we will hear of nothing else for days now."

I swallowed hard, my eyes inexplicably drawn to where the poor man lay on the ground.

Something far in the back of my mind flickered into life, like a spark when a stone strikes metal.

An image, hazy and dark, passed through my thoughts. It was brief, not more than a moment…but my heart lurched, aching as if it were being torn in two.

Unease coursed through my veins, making the small hairs at the back of my neck stand up. *Was that… a memory of some sort?*

And if it was, why was this whole ordeal bringing it to the forefront of my mind?

"Are you all right?" Lily asked, peering closely at me.

"Oh," I said, turning away, brushing some of the hair from my eyes. It had begun to slip out of its chignon since hurrying out of the house. "It's nothing. Really."

"You look rather pale all of a sudden," she said. She laid a hand on my arm. "I'm sure that Mr. Morton is quite all right. He likely drank himself into a stupor. I'm certain it isn't the first time."

I wanted to believe what she said, but the longer I stared at the concerned expressions of the men huddled over Mr. Morton, the less convinced of it I was.

Constable Brown left the group and walked briskly back over to us, his face solemn.

"Is he all right, Constable?" Lily asked.

He ignored the question and asked one of his own. "You said you saw him fall," he said, glancing between the two of us. "Did you happen to see anything that happened before he collapsed?"

"I didn't see anything," Lily said, laying a hand across her chest. Her head swiveled around and looked at me, her gaze piercing. "You were still sitting by the window, Iris, weren't you? What did you see?"

I froze, staring back and forth between her and the Constable.

That same icy fear flooded my veins, and my knees grew weak.

"I – " I said.

What am I to say? That I witnessed a shadow? That I saw something that I cannot explain?

"Well?" Lily asked. "What did you see?"

"I – " I attempted again. "I'm not really sure what I saw…"

Constable Brown and Lily both waited another moment for me to elaborate.

My mind slowed down, becoming almost entirely

blank. I couldn't string a thought together, and the sheer weight of what I thought might have happened weighed so heavily upon me that I couldn't bring myself to admit it aloud without fear of sounding entirely ridiculous.

"Well, if you think of it, inform me at once," Constable Brown said. "It seems there were not many witnesses to what occurred, and any information at this point might be helpful."

He adjusted the collar of his frock coat. "Now, we need to clear this street," he said. "It would be best if you ladies were to return home."

"Very well, sir," Lily said. "Come along, Iris. We don't wish to be in the way now, do we?"

I shook my head, and followed after Lily as she turned to head back toward our home.

I fought the urge, but lost just before we passed over the threshold of our front door, to look back at Mr. Morton once again.

I caught sight of his open hand lying stretched out. Not moving. Appearing…lifeless.

I suppressed a shudder.

"Iris, are you coming?" Lily asked from the other side of the door. "You are going to let in that horrid draft."

"I'm sorry," I said, and dashed inside after her, finally tearing my eyes away from the horror that seemed to have found its way into our small town.

3

"What is the matter with you?"

We had not been upstairs in our rooms for more than a moment before Lily rounded on me, hands planted firmly on her hips, her eyes blazing.

I flinched, my back to her as I pulled the shawl from my arms. It had been many years since she had used that tone of voice with me…likely not since I was fifteen or sixteen years old and had managed to spill a bottle of perfume on a dress she had been working on for a customer.

"What do you mean?" I asked, turning around slowly, my face as sheepish as I felt.

She huffed, rolling her eyes. "For goodness sake, Iris. The way you froze out there in front of the Constable? He asked you a very simple question, did he not?"

"The question may have been simple, but the

answer certainly wasn't," I said, folding the shawl over my arm. "I did not want to appear foolish."

"Well, you did," Lily snapped. "By *not* answering him, by clamming up like a frightened child, you made us both look foolish."

Blood rushed to my cheeks. "That is always your concern, isn't it?" I asked, my eyes narrowing. "Lily, I *was* frightened. How could I not be?"

"Why on earth were you frightened?" she asked. "Those men will give Mr. Morton whatever assistance he needs."

"*Lily*," I said, through clenched teeth. "Mr. Morton...I think he was – "

"What?" Lily snapped, folding her arms once again.

"He is dead!" I exclaimed, unable to hold it in any longer, the worst bursting from me.

Silence fell between us, the sound of the ticking clock on the mantel the only reminder that the whole world had not stopped in that moment.

"Why do you think that?" Lily asked. Some of the anger had been washed away, and fear had taken its place; I noticed the color had drained from her face, even in the dim light from the fireplace.

"Because I – " I said, my throat growing tight. I attempted to swallow past the lump that had formed there. "I saw a shadow come up behind him, and then he – he just collapsed. He stopped singing, and he fell to the ground like a ragdoll, his body limp and – "

"Just one moment," Lily said, holding up her

hands, shaking her head. "A *shadow* came up behind him? And what? Struck him?"

"I don't know," I said. "I couldn't even be sure that I was truly seeing what I believed I was seeing. How was I supposed to admit that to Constable Brown?"

Lily pursed her lips, looking away. A distant, yet focused gaze passed over her face.

"What is it?" I asked.

"Well, I don't imagine you really believe it was a *shadow* that might have attacked Mr. Morton."

"Whatever it was *did* attack him, Lily," I said. "Otherwise he would not have collapsed in the middle of the street the way he did."

Lily nodded sympathetically. "Very well. Yes, you are correct. But are you assuming that he was killed?"

"That is the only conclusion I can think of," I said.

Lily's eyes narrowed. "That would explain your troubled expression when you stood at the window…"

"Yes," I said.

The flicker of a memory passed through my mind once more. At least I thought it could be a memory. It was so brief, so dark. There were no sounds, no faces. I recognized nothing apart from a feeling deep in my very soul. Pure, unadulterated *fear*.

"It frightened me, Lily," I said in a low murmur, wrapping my arms around myself, chilled to the very bone.

Lily exhaled slowly. "Anyone would be frightened had they witnessed something as grave as you have," she said.

I swallowed, my mouth still incredibly dry, yet I knew my stomach would willingly reject anything I might try to put past my lips.

"Yet Constable Brown said nothing about Mr. Morton being dead..." Lily said, scratching her chin thoughtfully. "We asked him quite clearly what had occurred. If Mr. Morton is truly dead, then he should have been more forthcoming with us."

"I imagine he will be, once he is able to discern exactly what happened," I said. "Which is why he was asking us what we saw."

"Your testimony may have proven quite useful," Lily said. "Even still..."

She glanced toward the kitchen before coming over to me and taking my shawl from me.

"You sit," she said, pointing toward a chair beside the fire. "I shall make us some tea. I think we need it after everything we have experienced tonight. And I should like to hear precisely what it was that you saw that makes you think he might have been killed."

We sipped our tea together, and I told her everything I witnessed, even if it sounded rather ridiculous. As I retold it, I realized how bizarre it sounded. How could I have seen a shadow attack him like I had thought I had?

"It isn't entirely strange," Lily said. "Though the shadow you saw was, of course, a person. Someone who did not wish to be discovered. Likely wearing a disguise."

"A disguise?" I asked.

"Whoever it was must have been waiting in ambush, knowing that Mr. Morton would walk by eventually, yes?" Lily asked.

"I suppose…" I said. "But that thought is even more troubling. That would mean whoever attacked him had planned for this to happen."

"Indeed," Lily said, pursing her lips.

I breathed in the steam from my teacup, looking into its amber depths. "It's quite sad, really…Mr. Morton didn't deserve to die. Especially not in this way."

"No one deserves that," Lily said. "It is very sad."

I swirled the spoon in my cup, having mixed in another cube of sugar. "I remember when his business closed," I said. "It was such a sad day. That was Abigail's favorite place to go when she was young."

"Yes, and our cousin had quite expensive taste, as well," Lily said with a small smirk. "But I do remember. His toys were beautiful. Especially the rocking horses… I remember you mentioning them earlier. It has been a long time since I have thought of them…"

"Why did he have to close his shop?" I asked.

"Too many people were not purchasing his toys," Lily said. "I believe they became too expensive for most." She shook her head. "He simply didn't want to admit defeat, but he was unable to pay his bills. His entire livelihood was that store, but it wasn't bringing in enough money."

"That's terrible," I said. "Wasn't it his father's business before?"

Lily nodded. "Yes, and his father's before that."

I frowned. "And then after he had to close his business, his wife deserted him, correct?"

Lily nodded again. "Yes. Two years ago, now."

"Two years..." I said. "It's hard to believe it has been that long."

"It isn't without her constant reminder of the fact," Lily said. "Every time I see her, she makes a point to remind everyone that her fool of a husband ruined their finances, and that she might have made something of her life if her husband had not wasted his on a failing business. She has always been a rather proud and vindictive woman, you know."

"With his business having failed and his wife unwilling to live under the same roof with him, I suppose it is no wonder that he turned to drink," I said.

"To be perfectly honest, I almost wonder if Henrietta Morton tired of simply complaining about her husband and decided to end his life and finally be fully free of him," Lily said.

"Why?" I asked. "Hating him is one thing...but killing him? She doesn't strike me as someone who would be capable of something like that."

"I do not know her well enough to discern whether or not she would be," Lily said. "If it was purely out of spite..."

"Spite is not a reason to kill someone," I said.

"Perhaps in your mind," Lily said. "But we cannot assume that someone who *is* capable of murder is in their right mind in the first place. I would have to assume that they most certainly were not."

"I suppose you are right," I said, suppressing a shiver.

Lily peered into her own teacup. "It's all very unfortunate. The idea of someone in this town so upset that they would go so far as to kill another human being?" She scowled. "This just won't do. We cannot live in a place where people like this exist."

"What are you suggesting?" I asked.

Lily sighed. "I don't know, but I imagine we will not be the only ones who feel this way. In fact, as soon as the news spreads that Mr. Morton was killed, I am certain there will be a village uproar, as people demand that the culprit be caught."

"And you believe it could be Henrietta Morton?" I asked tentatively. "Even saying that out loud makes me feel rather queasy…"

"I understand," Lily said. "I never would have imagined it of anyone in this town, even Henrietta."

"I realize that most people find her a heartless sort of person, embittered by the ruin of her reputation. Still, it all seems rather unthinkable…" I said.

Lily shook her head. "I must admit, I do not like thinking this deeply about such matters. It delves into the parts of this world that I would rather not admit exist."

"What do you mean?" I asked.

Lily looked up at me, and I recognized the seriousness in her face. "The depths of the darkness of man, their depravity, their unthinkable ways..."

I felt the small hairs on my arms rise up in response. "It is disturbing to realize such people and actions exist..."

"We live quite removed from such horrors here," Lily said. "If we were in a larger place like London, we would be exposed to it a great deal more. I, for one, would despise that. I'm quite fond of our quiet life in Grangehurst."

"As am I," I said.

"Which is why I hope that Constable Brown will be able to find the truth," Lily said.

She gave me a pointed look.

"And I am afraid he won't be able to unless you tell him everything that you told me."

I swallowed hard, looking back at her.

"You're right," I said. "I suppose I should go speak with him."

"It can wait until morning," Lily said, getting to her feet. "For now, you need rest. It's been a shocking night for you, and the very last thing you need is to rob yourself of sleep with all these horrid ideas."

"Yes, I suppose you're right," I said, getting up after her.

I certainly hope the nightmares don't follow me to bed... I don't think I could bear it.

I frowned as Lily turned her back.

Something told me this was not the last I would see of the whole business.

4

I had never been very fond of sleep. Even as a young girl, I would sometimes wake in the middle of the night, tears streaming down my face, my throat raw from screaming myself hoarse as a result of the darkness that seemed to permeate my mind as soon as I fell asleep.

I never knew what the nightmares were about, which was equally as frustrating. Lily told me that children would often experience these night terrors, with shapes and shadows of the unknown. She often explained that it was a result of growing up, of losing the innocence of childhood when our fragile minds were exposed to the more adult parts of this life.

It made perfect sense to me, though I did wonder why the fears of childhood followed me through to my young adulthood, and further. I was to turn thirty very soon, and I still felt the tangles of the wicked web of nightmares.

As such, I endeavored to keep them to myself. It had almost come to a point where I was utterly used to these dreams. I expected them. Lily didn't know, though. Ever since I turned seventeen and she told me that I should not still be having the dreams of a child, and she gave me books to read before I went to sleep in order to distract my mind.

When she asked me if that had solved my problems, I had lied and said it had. She seemed pleased, and more than that, relieved.

I, however, continued to suffer, night after night.

The night that we saw Mr. Morton collapse in the street, however…that was a night when I realized my dreams had changed from those of a child…to the nightmares of an adult who had witnessed death.

I dreamt of darkness and shadows, and hovering shapes at the edge of my vision. Every time I turned my head, a person was just out of sight, slipping out of my view, leaving me with a sinking heaviness.

I WOKE BEFORE THE SUNRISE, well before dawn, lying in my bed in a cold sweat. I flinched at every sound, while Lily's gentle breathing counted the moments that I remained awake.

Eventually, I realized that I was not going to be able to fall back asleep, as any peace had escaped me. I rose as quietly as I could, dressed, and made my way to the kitchen. I considered making myself something for breakfast, but even the thought of something as simple as bread and cheese made my stomach turn.

I glanced at the clock. It was nearly five in the morning.

I'm certain Constable Brown will be awake in these early hours. Perhaps I should go visit him, alleviate some of the distress that seems to have draped itself upon me.

A brief opening of the front door told me that the temperature had dropped quite significantly during the night, and sent me looking for a warmer hat, scarf, and gloves in the closet. I settled on a matching set that Lily had made for me for Christmas the year before, a beautiful plum purple fabric which had cost her likely far too much.

I glanced at the door leading up to our rooms, and sighed. She would likely be nervous, finding my bed empty, until she went to the kitchen and discovered the note I'd left for her. I explained that I intended to speak to the Constable as early as possible, and that I would return home after seeing him. It would make her feel much better, I was certain, to put this all behind us. She would also be happy to know that I would be avoiding gossip as well, going well before the town woke for the day.

I stepped outside, breathing in deeply. The dull, grey light of dawn had begun to peek through the trees, bathing the world in a foggy gloominess.

Few sounds greeted me; the cluck of chickens from Miss Violet's back garden, the clang of the bell down at the fishing wharf, and the rush of the wind through the trees.

The cold air made my eyes weep, and I squinted against the breeze brushing across my face. I pulled my cloak more tightly over my shoulders, and glanced down the street.

The skin prickled at the base of my skull as my eyes fell upon the part of the street where Mr. Morton had fallen the night before. It wasn't any different than it typically was. There were no marks indicating that anything had taken place. No discoloration. No signs. I could see nothing that would tell any passersby that he had collapsed in that precise place.

I felt a twisting in my stomach as I thought of people walking right over that place without a second thought. Children with a cheerful skip in their step, adults hurrying about their days...

Would anyone look at that place in the road the same way I did? Would anyone ever remember it?

I turned and scolded myself. *It will not do to dwell on these travesties. All I am doing is wasting my own time, as well as the Constable's by delaying my report.*

I hoped that by my sharing what I had seen, he would be able to find the culprit, and put this terrible event out of our minds.

And more than that...I hope he will have good news to share with me, letting me know that Mr. Morton is, in fact, quite all right and only in need of some good, long rest.

Those thoughts encouraged me as I made my way up the street. Past the bakery, past the post office. I turned down off Front Street, heading east along Church Street.

The road wound upward along the hillsides, and I passed by the office where Doctor Webb worked, as well as the grocer's, *Tom's Premiere*. The church, a beautiful stone structure that had been standing for nearly seven hundred years, stood at the top of the hill overlooking the town. Adorned with a square tower at the back, and stained glass windows all around the outside which let in beautiful light during the services on Sunday morning, it was a hallmark of the town, and a piece of ancient history that had been painstakingly preserved.

At the end of the road, where Church Street gave way to Rowan Lane, there sat a small barn that had been converted to a station of sorts for the police and the fire brigade. Grangehurst was fortunate to have our own brigade, which also served the neighboring villages. The large doors made it easy for the firemen to remove their gear, and the top floor of the structure was where all the offices were held, including Constable Brown's.

I approached the door, hearing a grinding of metal on metal from inside the mouth of the barn, followed soon after by laughter from several men.

Preparing for their day, most likely. Or perhaps a change in shifts?

When I raised my hand to knock on the door, I found a face staring at me through the glass on the other side.

As he pulled open the door, I realized I didn't recognize him. He was quite young, perhaps only a few years older than I was. He had a kind face, with a strong jawline, thick chestnut eyebrows, and honey brown hair that hung around his ears and looked as if it needed a trim.

He wore a simple linen shirt, which he left unbuttoned at the throat, and navy, woolen trousers. Part of his fire brigade uniform. He either was just coming in to work, or perhaps was on his way home. It was difficult to tell, the way he rolled up his sleeves, and the brightness in his eyes, which were a steely blue.

"Good morning," he said, his voice deep and rich. "You are here quite early, aren't you?"

"I suppose I am," I said, glancing over my shoulder. The first golden light of dawn had begun to appear through the trees, but the sun still slumbered beneath the horizon. "I am here to see Constable Brown."

"Oh, well, of course," the young man said, standing back from the door to allow me to pass. "He arrived just a quarter of an hour ago. Your timing is impeccable."

I stepped through, and caught the scent of pine and firewood smoke as I passed by the man. It was rather pleasant.

"I must apologize, Miss, but I do not believe we have met yet," he said, falling into step beside me as we headed toward the stairs to the offices upstairs. "Which isn't of great surprise, as I am new to Grangehurst."

"Oh," I said.

"My name is Nash. Nash Greenwood. I just moved here from Sheffield. I'm here to train some of the newer recruits to the fire brigade," he said.

"That's very good of you," I said. "My name is Iris Dickinson. My sister and I own the seamstress shop on Front Street."

"Oh!" he exclaimed. "Your sister must be Miss Lily, then?"

"Yes," I said. "Have you met her?"

He nodded, beginning to ascend the stairs beside me. "She was the one who finished my new tunic for my uniform. My old one needed some repairing, and she realized it would simply be easier to replace it all together."

"That sounds like Lily," I said. "Always the perfectionist."

Nash grinned, and I felt my cheeks flush ever so slightly. How long had it been since a handsome young man had smiled at me like that? "She did an excellent job," he said. "Better than my original, and the chief was all too pleased with it."

"Well, I'm glad to hear it," I said. "I'm certain she will be as well, when I tell her."

"Oh, good, yes, please do tell her," he said.

We reached the landing.

"Well, it was very nice to meet you, Miss Dickinson," Nash said with a small bow. "I must return to the rest of the brigade, as we have intense training planned today. I thought we might take advantage of the cold weather and work down by the water."

"Won't the poor brigadiers catch their death?" I asked.

"They won't if they follow my instructions," Nash said with a small wink and a smile.

With that, he turned and hurried back down the stairs, humming a verse of a hymn that seemed to tug at my memories, as I was unable to place it with the few notes he had sung.

He had left me in front of the door with a placard beside it, reading *Constable William D. Brown.*

Nervousness washed over me once again as I raised my hand to knock.

"Come in," I heard the Constable say in his somewhat gruff voice.

I found him sitting at his desk as I pushed open the door. He sat in front of a pile of papers, all of which were seemingly out of order, spread out over the desk, covering the entire surface.

He glanced up at me as I entered, blinking his icy blue eyes. "Oh, Miss Iris," he said, running his fingers over his sandy beard. He leaned back in his seat. "What can I do for you at such an early hour?"

As I stepped more fully into the office, I noticed the dark circles under his eyes. *Did the poor man sleep at all last night?* His shirt, also, was the same one he had been wearing the night before when we saw him.

"I wanted to apologize first," I said. "For behaving as strangely as I did last night. I suppose the whole ordeal rather frightened me, and that made it hard for me to think clearly when you asked me about what I had seen."

He patiently waited for me to continue. I imagined he might not have a great deal of patience left after being awake all night, as I suspected he might have been.

"I felt terrible about it, and so decided it was best to come and tell you what I could remember as early as I could," I said.

Constable Brown nodded his head, and rose to move a wooden chair that sat against the wall beside the door in front of his desk. "Here," he said. "Have a seat. Shall I fetch us some tea?"

"That would be lovely, yes," I said.

He nodded once again and excused himself from the room.

I settled myself into the chair, my heart attempting to rise into my throat. I did my best to take long, slow breaths to calm myself, but the memories of the night before had begun to bounce around inside my mind once again, and I feared I might clam up again when attempting to describe it to him.

No. I have come all this way. I will tell him what I saw, and I shall leave this all in his capable hands. As soon as I am able to get these terrible feelings off my chest, then it will be his responsibility, not mine.

I resolved to look around the room in order to distract myself as I waited for the Constable to return with our tea.

His office, while quite small in size, was welcoming.

He had a portrait of him and his family on the wall beside the door, and another, smaller portrait of his four children that hung on the wall beside the tall bookshelf that sat behind him. A potted plant was in the window, and appeared quite lovingly cared for. Was the Constable a green thumb secretly?

"Here we are," came his voice as he entered the room once again. "Thankfully, Mr. Riley just made a fresh pot. Would you care for sugar in your tea?"

"Yes, please," I said. "My sister scolds me for how much I enjoy sugar in my tea."

Constable Brown chuckled. "Never fear, my wife feels the same about me. She tells me that I may as well fill my teacup with sweets."

I smiled.

He set the teacup down in front of me, and I took it gratefully. I closed my cold fingers around the warm ceramic, and the nervousness began to ease in my soul.

He sat down across from me, exhaling heavily as he did. "Well, Miss Iris...why don't you tell me what you managed to see last night?"

I stared down at my cup, the anxiousness returning ever so slightly.

"Well..." I said. "We heard Mr. Morton outside last night. It certainly was not the first time, as we have heard him carrying on as he made his way home from the pub before. It was quite clear he had had too much to drink, as I watched him stumble down the street. He even began to sing a sea shanty..."

I swallowed hard as the memories pressed against

my mind, as if trying to force their way inside, angry and frightening.

"And then I – " I said, looking away. I felt foolish even saying it again. "I saw a shadow appear behind him as he walked between the lights of the lampposts. He reappeared in the next halo of light, but the shadow followed. I watched as it rushed up to him, and then Mr. Morton went silent, and fell to the ground."

Constable Brown's neutral expression suddenly became concerned. He leaned forward in his seat and looked at me very closely. "A shadow, you say?" he asked.

I nodded. "Yes, sir. A shadow. A silhouette of some sort."

"Did you manage to see any particular shape?" he asked. "What about the height of the shadow? The weight?"

I shook my head. "None of those things were clear to me. It didn't seem a great deal taller than Mr. Morton, but it moved so fast that it was quite hard to tell..."

"Hmm..." Constable Brown said, sitting back in his seat. He ran his fingers through his beard once more. "You are the only one to mention another person at the scene...it would make sense, though, given how quickly he collapsed..."

"I was the only one to see it?" I asked, my stomach sinking. "Well, that could mean I didn't see anything at all. As I said, it was dark, and we were up in our rooms, well above the street. It could have been nothing more than a trick of the light, or – "

"Why do you doubt yourself?" Constable Brown asked. "I can see from your face that you truly believe you saw what you saw. And I have no reason to believe that you would lie about something like this, especially given the circumstances."

"No, I certainly am not lying," I said. "But to be the only one to have seen it – "

"I am pleased that you chose to come to me after all," he said. "I know it must have been frightening for you. Of course, I wish that you had managed to see more detail, as a shadowy figure alone is not enough to help us discern who it might have been."

I licked my lips, my conversation with Lily the night before coming back to me.

"The trouble is, Mr. Morton's reputation hasn't been the best these past few years," Constable Brown said, bringing his tea to his lips, sipping thoughtfully. "If anything, he has likely made more enemies than friends in his current state. I have been dragged down to the pub on more than one occasion to pull him off some poor fellow who might have insulted him. He never remembered it, of course, even if he woke up in a cell."

He shook his head, regarding his teacup with pity.

"I always felt rather sorry for the poor fellow," he said. "His business failing, his wife gone, taking the children with her…"

He glanced up at the portrait of his own family on the wall.

"I can't imagine what that must have been like for him."

"Quite troubling, I imagine," I said.

"Yes, indeed," he said.

"I..." I began, nervous once again. "I don't mean to insinuate that I know anything, but is it possible that it was his wife?"

Constable Brown looked up at me, his eyes narrowing as he considered what I had said. "Mrs. Morton?" he asked. He ran his fingers through his beard once again, whistling through the gap in his front teeth. "Well, she was the first suspect I considered, of course, given their sordid history..."

My heart skipped. Was it possible that Lily's theory was correct?

I suppose it shouldn't come as such a shock to me... Lily is always so level-headed, so logical...isn't that just the sort of person who could figure these sorts of problems out?

He sighed once again, setting down his teacup, nearly empty. "It's difficult to say, however. It certainly warrants investigation..." He massaged the narrow bridge of his nose. "It was the most difficult news to tell her this morning. I stopped there just before coming to the station here. But she – "

"So he – " I said, still trying to fully absorb the idea. "He really is...?"

"Dead?" Constable Brown asked. He looked down,

averting his eyes. "Yes. I imagine that the moment he collapsed was when his death occurred."

A chill ran down my spine. *The moment I saw him fall...that was when he passed on?*

Why did I have to see the exact moment it happened?

"As I was saying, I suspected the same as you, that perhaps she had some involvement. However, when I went to tell her the news this morning, it turns out that she wasn't even home. According to Mrs. Hobbs, she hasn't been home for some time. It seems she and the children had gone to visit a cousin out of town, and wouldn't be back for at least another week." He shook his head. "This is not the sort of news that I like to put in a letter, but it is more important that she hear what occurred, rather than how she hears it, I suppose."

"What if the neighbor was lying?" I asked. "Or is it possible that Henrietta – I mean, Mrs. Morton – was lying?"

"Oh, it is certainly possible," Constable Brown said. "I have no intentions of completely writing her off until she returns home and I have a chance to speak with her myself. It seemed quite convenient that she happened to be out of town when her husband passed away."

I chewed the inside of my lip. This was all deeply troubling, and I found myself frustrated that it seemed to be unfolding around me.

"Well, I am sorry to involve you in all this," Constable Brown said. "I've likely said too much already, but I am thankful that you came and told me what you managed to see last night. I imagine it will prove useful to our investigation. Now, may I walk you – "

The door to his office flew open, banging against the back wall.

I whirled around in my chair, and was surprised to see Doctor Webb standing on the threshold.

A man easily twice the age of Constable Brown, he was as frail as he was ornery. The sort of man with little bedside manner, he was still the most skilled physician for many miles around. People would come to him from all over Yorkshire to receive his keen diagnoses and treatments.

His hair, wooly and white, stuck out at odd angles around his head and his blue eyes appeared bulbous behind the thick lenses in his spectacles. The wrinkles near his eyes deepened as he squinted at Constable Brown.

"Constable," he said, stepping inside, right past me, completely ignoring me. "You will not believe what I have discovered."

"I'm certain that whatever it is you must tell me is fascinating," Constable Brown said. "However, I was just – "

"Fascinating does not even begin to describe it," Doctor Webb said, leaning against the desk, once again entirely unaware of my presence. "It will change the whole course of the investigation, of that I am certain."

Constable Brown gave me a wary look before

returning to Doctor Webb. "The investigation? Doctor, couldn't we – "

"It seems that it wasn't an attacker that killed poor Mr. Morton," Doctor Webb said, continuing on as if Constable Brown had said nothing.

"I – what?" Constable Brown asked, eyes narrowing. "How is that possible – "

"Poison," Doctor Webb said with a self-satisfied, low chuckle. "It was poison, it was."

The astonishment was clear on Constable Brown's face. "What?" he breathed.

Doctor Webb nodded. "And what a bizarre poison it was. Masterfully engineered, not the result of some accident. This was intentional, meant to kill, meant to – "

Doctor Webb halted his explanation, following Constable Brown's gaze...which was fixed pointedly upon me.

As soon as Doctor Webb saw me, his already enormous eyes widened even further, giving him the appearance of an enlarged fly.

"Oh, good heavens," he said. "What a fool I am."

5

Doctor Webb and Constable Brown regarded me as if I were some sort of stranger, sitting there in the room with them, as if I had suddenly appeared out of thin air, or perhaps had snuck in without their knowing.

Constable Brown cleared his throat. "Well...Doctor Webb, if you would wait right here for a moment, I shall walk Miss Dickinson out, and we can discuss this...revelation further."

Doctor Webb nodded his head, his frizzled white hair bouncing as he did so. "My apologies, Miss Dickinson, I did not see you sitting there."

Clearly.

I rose from my seat, realizing that I had now overstayed my welcome.

Constable Brown did not make eye contact with me as we stepped out of the office. He closed his door behind himself, turning to me.

"Thank you once again for bringing your information in to me," he said. "It was very brave of you to do so, especially given how frightened you must have been. I hope you will find peace in knowing that your testimony may help us uncover what happened."

I nodded. "I am glad I was able to help."

Constable Brown glanced up and down the hall before leaning in a bit closer. He dropped his voice as he spoke. "I would appreciate it greatly if you weren't to repeat what Doctor Webb said just a moment ago. This information should remain...discreet until we have uncovered the full truth about what happened to Mr. Morton. You understand."

"Oh, of course," I said. "I understand completely."

"Very good," he said with a firm nod. "I hope I haven't taken up too much time in your day, Miss Dickinson."

He speaks as if it were his fault that I chose to come and speak with him today.

"Not at all, Constable," I said.

"Have a pleasant day, then," he said, and walked back into his office, closing the door behind him.

It makes perfect sense that he would be eager to question the doctor...or to scold him for being so foolish as to speak without checking to see if they were alone or not.

I made my way back down the stairs, glancing briefly toward the door leading to the barn proper. I heard muffled voices inside still, so it was likely that Nash Greenwood and the other brigadiers had not gone down to the river for their training.

He certainly was friendly. I imagine he will find he likes it here in Grangehurst.

I hurried back to the shop, only to find that it had been open for nearly a half hour when I arrived.

"I am terribly sorry," I said to Lily as I tugged the gloves off my fingers. "I hadn't realized it was so late."

"It's perfectly all right," Lily said, though her tone was a bit sharp. "But I need you to locate Miss Violet's order. She will be here within the hour to collect it."

The day began as most typically did, with Lily taking inventory of what materials we had to begin new orders, allowing me to take the time to sort through orders to be delivered or picked up, ready and waiting for their owners.

"Oh, it's stunning," Mrs. Clark said just before noon as she examined the dress that Lily had finished for her. She ran her fingers over the silky, green fabric, her eyes wide. "It's more beautiful than anything I could have ever imagined."

"You will surely be the loveliest lady at the dinner party this weekend," I said. "Mr. Clark will be smitten all over again, I'm certain of it."

She beamed at me. "Thank you. And thank you, Miss Lily. You ladies always go far above and beyond."

I smiled. "You are quite welcome."

"Yes, you are welcome, indeed," Lily said from beside me.

Mrs. Clark made her way out of the store, staring in adoration at the gown.

I glanced over at Lily as Mrs. Clark stepped outside. "All finished with that hem?"

"Nearly," Lily said, pulling a box of miscellaneous buttons from beneath the counter. "It's just missing something…I can't quite put my finger on what it is…"

My eyes swept through the store. A few customers lingered near the front, browsing through the swatches of fabric we had for dress orders, or examining the buttons that we could order for custom requests.

"So…when are you going to tell me what Constable Brown said this morning?" Lily asked, dropping her voice as she pieced through the box.

I glanced over at her. She had not met my gaze, and kept her voice low enough so as to not attract the gaze of the customers. "Oh, yes…" I said.

We hadn't had more than a moment to speak with one another since I returned home, and those conversations had been about nothing more than the orders or people's requests as they came and went.

"Did you tell him everything you told me?" she asked, shaking the box, unearthing some of the buttons toward the bottom.

I licked my lips. "Yes," I said. "Though I don't know what good it will do him, as I knew nothing of the attacker apart from the fact he or she was a shadow."

Lily looked up at me. "Did he already know that?"

I shook my head. "No, but he wished I could have told him how tall the person was, or how much they might have weighed. As it is, all he knows is that Mr. Morton was attacked."

My heart skipped, and I leaned forward, closer to her. Dropping my voice slightly, I spoke again. "And not only that, but as I was speaking with the Constable, Doctor Webb burst into the room, only to inform the Constable that Mr. Morton seems to have been killed by poisoning. He said it was a very strange sort of poison as well, one that he had not ever – "

"Shh," Lily snapped.

Her eyes darted toward the door, which had just closed.

I had not even heard it open.

I realized quickly, however, what it was that Lily was staring at. Or rather…who.

Mrs. Minford stood there, her eyes glued to the two of us.

Oh, no…she heard us, didn't she?

For a moment, we could only stare across the short distance at her, standing frigidly beside one another.

"You're speaking of Mr. Morton, aren't you?" she asked, her eyes narrowed, her mouth curling into a mischievous grin.

Lily gave me a sharp jab in the ribs with her elbow, which she deftly covered by pretending to adjust the apron she wore around her waist. "What of Mr. Morton?" she asked, giving Mrs. Minford a blank look as she picked up the order book, beginning to page through it.

Mrs. Minford eagerly stepped forward, her eyes

darting back and forth between Lily and I. "I heard you mention his name," she said, staring intently up at me, eyes widening. "What have you heard?"

I nervously glanced over at Lily, which I realized at once was a mistake. It made me look as guilty as I felt.

She stepped up to the counter. "Oh, come now, everyone is talking about it," she said. "I saw you both standing out there in the street last night. Constable Brown even spoke with you, didn't he? What did he say? Does he know what happened?"

"We don't know anything," Lily said, rather curtly. "This is a matter best handled by Constable Brown, and I intend to let him be the one who will resolve it."

"Oh, I couldn't agree more," Mrs. Minford said with a firm nod. "But isn't it quite strange how it all occurred? After dark, right in the middle of the street? It makes one wonder if his heart failed him, or perhaps some other sort of health trouble..."

She looked carefully between Lily and me, her gaze searching our expressions for confirmation.

My face burned as I attempted to busy myself with something else, just as Lily did. Nothing seemed quite right, though, so I settled on examining one of the stacks of swatches I had set beside the order book for Lily to look through.

"If I'm not mistaken," Mrs. Minford said, leaning forward across the counter, her eyes carefully sweeping across the store. "I thought I heard you say something...about poisoning?"

There weren't many customers, but I noticed a few

shooting glances over at us; Mrs. Minford certainly was not trying especially hard to keep her voice down.

My face flooded with color, and I did my best to stare down at the robin's egg blue swatch in my hands with great intensity; *Now, wouldn't this be a lovely scarf? Or perhaps a pair of gloves?*

"Come now, ladies…" Mrs. Minford said. "You can tell me. Whatever is said will stay between us, of course."

Lily stiffened beside me as she forcefully turned the page on the order book. "I'm sorry, Mrs. Minford, but I believe you were mistaken. We haven't heard anything about – "

"Because if you *did* happen to mention poisoning, it would certainly make sense," she said. "Given the way the poor man collapsed. And there wasn't any blood, no visible wounds…how else might he have died? A blow to the head? But again, I've heard there were no external injuries."

She scratched her chin, staring absently down at the counter. "I imagine someone had it out for poor Mr. Morton. His death has really taken quite a toll on the community. And I'm certain everyone knows about it by now. How could one not, when something so tragic happened right outside in the middle of the street?"

My heart had taken residence in my throat, making it difficult for me to breathe. I did my best to keep as calm and collected as possible. More than anything, I wanted to be away from this conversation.

I turned and tried to walk away, but Mrs. Minford's question held me in place.

"What did Doctor Webb say, exactly? When he came into the Constable's office? And what did you see that you had to go speak with him today?"

I bit down on my lip, trying to keep calm.

I turned and looked at Lily, who was giving me a stern look, as if to say *Perhaps we should have waited to have this conversation later...*

"I – " I said.

Lily, however, jumped into the conversation for me.

"I am sorry, Mrs. Minford, but Iris did not see anything that would help explain what happened to the unfortunate Mr. Morton," she said. "She went to the Constable this morning to answer his questions when she had been far too overwhelmed last night to do so. Why would he have any reason to tell her anything about what happened? It is a police matter."

Mrs. Minford nodded. "Yes, I suppose you are right," she said, looking skeptically at me. "However...if it really was a poisoning...then I imagine there is only one source where a poison could have come from."

"Oh?" Lily asked in her least enthusiastic tone.

Mrs. Minford nodded. "Of course. If the poisoning was something strange to the Doctor, then it likely came from somewhere unknown to him, correct? That would mean there is only one person who could be responsible."

"And who would that be?" Lily asked.

Mrs. Minford gave her a frustrated look. "Why,

Captain Seymour, of course. He must have brought the poison back with him from India."

6

"Captain Seymour?" Lily repeated many hours later as she slid the lock home on the front door of our shop. She shook her head in disgust, letting out a heavy sigh.

"What about him?" I asked, folding up a large sample of muslin that one of our customers had been looking at earlier.

"Mrs. Minford..." Lily said, planting her hands on her hips as she looked over at me. "Somehow she managed to walk in at precisely the time you were beginning to tell me about what happened when you went to visit Constable Brown today. How is it that woman is always at the least convenient places at the worst times?"

"I'm sorry," I said. "I do feel as if the whole matter is my fault."

Lily sighed, spinning the *Open* sign around, the *Closed* side now facing the street. "I am not upset with you," she said. "Though it might have been wise to use some discretion. I am simply aggravated at her usual insistence on knowing every little detail about the lives of her neighbors. Does the woman not have her own matters to be getting on with?"

"She will have likely started some ridiculous rumor all on her own," I said. "It sounded as if she was already trying to develop one before she ever heard what I said."

Lily walked back to the counter, where she began to hang bolts of fabric back into their designated places along the wall. All of them had been used, measured, or examined that day. I watched as she scrawled down notes about which we needed to order more of before returning them to their places. "I suppose you are correct," she continued. "The woman never would have let that much time pass before she was involved in the whole affair somehow, some way... as aggravating as that is."

She hung the last bolt on the wall, dusting her hands off, regarding it with a great deal of distaste.

"And from what she said, almost everyone in town had heard about the death by this morning. I cannot say I am all too surprised, but what she failed to mention was whether or not she was the one who went door to door to inform everyone," Lily said, glancing over her shoulder at me. "It would not take a great deal of imagination to envision that, would it?"

"Perhaps not," I said, rolling up a spool of green

thread that had bounced onto the ground during one of the fittings that afternoon.

"What was it Doctor Webb said, then?" Lily asked. "Since Mrs. Minford seemed intent on interrupting us as thoroughly as she did?"

I set the rerolled spool down, stooping then to fetch the shears that Lily had been using with it. "Well, it wasn't a great deal," I said. "Constable Brown told me more than I believe he meant to, confirming that Mr. Morton was indeed dead, and I shared with him our theory about it possibly being his wife – "

"You told him what we discussed?" Lily asked, eyes narrowing. "Iris, I do not wish to involve myself in this business more than we already have."

"I didn't mention you," I said. "I simply asked if it was possible that it was her. He said he already had considered it, but having gone to visit her this morning to tell her the news, he found that she and her children are supposedly out of town."

"Why do you say it like that?" Lily asked. "*Supposedly?* Does the Constable think that could be false information?"

I said, "It was given to him by one of her neighbors, but he wonders if it was somehow a cover story for her."

"That's troubling," Lily said, with a frown.

I nodded. "Yes, I thought the same. He said he would not dismiss her as a suspect until after he had a chance to speak with her upon her return home."

"That seems logical," Lily said. "And then Doctor Webb?"

"Yes, that...Well, Constable Brown was just readying himself to walk me out when Doctor Webb burst into the room, claiming he had discovered what happened to Mr. Morton, saying that it was poison. And not just poison. He described it as bizarre, and said it was, '*Masterfully engineered, not the result of some accident. This was intentional, meant to kill, meant to...*'"

I shrugged. "That was when he realized I was sitting in the room with the Constable, and he felt rather foolish for speaking too much."

"Ah..." Lily said. "Well, that is very unfortunate for Mr. Morton, of course, though I must admit that I am pleased to see Doctor Webb and the Constable working so diligently to locate the person responsible."

I ran my fingers over the back of one of the chairs set up near the fitting area, my nail finding the groove of the leaves carved into the wood as it always tended to, tracing the familiar shape. "What do you think of Mrs. Minford's theory, then? Do you think she could be right?"

"Captain Seymour..." Lily said, staring absently into the distance. "Yes, well...I'm not sure. He returned to Grangehurst after his service in India, so it's safe to assume that he likely brought mementos from his time there home with him. Would that mean he would bring a poison back with him? And, a greater question than even that...why would someone like him go after a man like Mr. Morton? Did they know one another prior to his serving in the military overseas? Did something happen between them more recently?"

Lily shook her head, looking disgusted with herself once again. "No," she said, holding up a hand. "This is already far more invested in the matter than I ever wanted to be."

She looked up at me, an expression of determination on her face. "We must agree to put this behind us," she said. "I realize it will be difficult, given the likelihood of it being discussed around town, especially until the attacker is located...but it will do nothing good for you. For either of us. It is best if we move on, forget about the unfortunate Mr. Morton, and say a prayer for his family. Apart from that, we can do little else. Why trouble ourselves with something as abhorrent as murder? If nothing else, it would make us appear to be a pair of idle gossips just as much as Mrs. Minford."

"You are right, sister," I said. The idea of being seen as a prying busybody was enough to sober me, but that did not prevent my mind from washing over the information for the rest of the evening.

I tried my hand at needlepoint once again, but found it hard to concentrate on the task at hand. My thoughts drifted toward Captain Seymour, and whether or not it really could have been him who killed poor Mr. Morton.

It is quite hard to imagine putting a face with the identity of someone capable of killing a man. I simply cannot imagine anyone in this town being capable of something so horrendous. And to use something as frightening as a poison? That would mean whoever it was that killed him did so methodically, had thought of it, considered it carefully...

I did my best to suppress the shivers that wanted to crawl up and down my spine every time I thought of Mr. Morton's body, lying there in the street...

But Captain Seymour? Could it *really* have been him?

We knew little about the man, which was odd, since he lived in the house directly across the street from our shop. It had been quiet for many years, and according to Mrs. Minford – was there anything about this town that the woman did *not* know? – it belonged to his family. He had been living on and off in London, being a part of the army, but a little over twenty years ago, he accepted a promotion, which required his serving nearly two decades in India. He returned home only a month or so ago, having retired from his time in the service.

Many people in town had known him, but his long absence had all but made him a stranger to most.

Strangers could certainly be frightening, but Captain Seymour always seemed kind to Lily and I. He was helpful, as well, offering to lift heavy orders and carry them inside for us.

He even offered to repair our broken front window just after we had been introduced to him, after some rambunctious youths had broken it with a rock. Lily was convinced that incident was accidental, but I was almost positive it was a reaction to her scolding the boys for being so disruptive as they played in the street.

Would he have access to some strange poisons? Doctor Webb said that it was bizarre, well made...would he even recognize something from such a distant place?

It still did not sit right with me that it could have been our neighbor.

But who am I to think that I am any judge of character? I hardly know the man, after all. Someone might appear perfectly friendly on the exterior, but heaven only knows the sort of person he could be on the inside...

Those thoughts troubled me, however.

Kindness is not something that one can easily pretend... at least not true, genuine kindness. And I do not think it is right or good for people to suspect him simply because he was gone for as long as he was, only having recently returned to town. What does it matter if he spent so long in India?

Yet Mrs. Minford did not seem particularly uncomfortable about accusing him, did she? She talked about it as easily as if she were describing the weather, or perhaps someone's choice in clothing.

What was it about him that made Mrs. Minford jump to that conclusion so readily? Was there something about him I didn't know? Something that she did?

"Iris?" Lily asked.

I looked up from my needlework, which had not changed in the last ten or so minutes. I had simply been staring down at it, thinking hard about Captain Seymour. "Yes?"

"Are you all right?" Lily asked, brow furrowing.

"Yes, quite fine," I said with a tight, quick smile, ducking my head to resume the needlepoint, which seemed a great deal less interesting now.

Lily's silent response told me she didn't fully believe me, but I ignored it. I didn't need her scolding me for dwelling on matters best left to the authorities.

THE NEXT MORNING, I found myself thinking about Mrs. Morton once again, Mr. Morton's wife, who had deserted him. She seemed a likely suspect, given her hatred of the man. Wouldn't that be a motivation for killing someone? Just because Captain Seymour might appear to have more of an opportunity to have such exotic poisons, did not mean he had motive.

"Miss Iris? Is everything all right?"

I blinked, coming back to myself.

I looked up, meeting Miss Baldwin's gaze in the reflection of the mirror.

I stood with a button between my teeth, the needle and thread in my hand poised to be used on the lower part of the wedding dress's sleeve.

"Oh!" I exclaimed. "I am terribly sorry, Miss Baldwin. I must have forgotten myself for a moment."

The young woman smiled at me sympathetically in the mirror. "Oh, it's quite all right," she said. "I feel the same way these days...it seems at the drop of a hat, I can forget what I am doing, or where I am supposed to be going." She glanced over her shoulder, looking right at the real me. "It happens when one has a great deal on one's mind."

"Yes…" I said. "I suppose it does."

"Yet one should do one's best to remain focused on the task at hand," said Lily, her stern reflection appearing beside me in the mirror.

I looked over at her, my cheeks turning pink. "I'm sorry," I said. "I'm really not sure what came over me."

Lily's brow arched. "Why don't you finish that button so Miss Baldwin can be on her way?"

"Of course," I said. "Right away."

I did, and the young woman was delighted with the work I had done for her. "Thank you so very much," she said. "This truly is the most beautiful gown I could have ever imagined. And I have you to thank for it. Both of you."

Lily rounded on me as soon as she went out of the shop. "Would you care to tell me what has you so preoccupied today?"

"I'm sorry, sister," I said. "I didn't mean for it to – "

"You are thinking about the business with Mr. Morton again, aren't you?" Lily asked, her eyes narrowing further.

I said, "I'm sorry, Lily, but it's very troubling to me. I witnessed his death, and it is difficult for me to think of happy things when I realize what a terrible night he had."

"I understand," Lily said, her tone relaxing a little. "But dwelling on death and misery is going to do nothing except distress you. I am not saying these things to be cruel, Iris. I am simply looking out for you. I know how sensitive you are, how troubling these sorts of events could be to you."

She was right, and I knew it. She meant no harm by it. "I do tend to hang onto distressing events, don't I?"

"Yes, you do," Lily said with a sigh.

She glanced up at the clock on the wall, which read half past two.

"Well…there are some things in town that I need, and I would rather not wait until market day to retrieve them. Perhaps the best thing that you could do is go outdoors, get some fresh air, and collect those items I need," she said.

"Are you certain you don't need my help here?" I asked. "I know that Mrs. Newman's order must be completed by next Tuesday, and we still have to finish the measurements for that."

"Yes, all that is true, but you are going to be of little help here for the time being, as distracted as you are," Lily said. "Let me fetch the list, and you can be on your way."

A FEW MINUTES LATER, I drew my walking cloak over my shoulders as I stepped outside, Lily's list clutched tightly in my hand.

The sun had finally made an appearance. The clouds overhead were thick and white, billowing like the sails of ships at sea. The air had a bite to it and the wind cut through the linen of the dress I wore quite easily, causing me to draw the cloak more tightly around myself.

Lily's last words hung over me like a storm cloud.

"There is work to be done," she had said. *"And you and I really cannot afford to dwell on these bizarre happenings. It may as well be one of those novels that you read."*

Those words hurt. Yet I could not dismiss the truth hiding in her statement.

She was right. The whole business seemed as farfetched as the stories I read, and it was infuriating to realize that I had become so consumed by it. Was there that little excitement in my life that I could think of nothing else?

I glanced down at the list in my hands, knowing Lily was only trying to protect me with her actions. Getting me out of the shop, giving me a chance to collect myself once again, clear my mind.

I looked up at the sign hanging over the front door of the shop, reading *The Golden Spool,* a name that Lily had come up with. Lily was responsible for everything we had in our lives. She started the business, she grew it entirely on her own. Because of her, we were the only independent women in town who owned a shop, which was a source of great pride for Lily, and as a result, brought great respect to us both, and our business.

She proves time and again that she doesn't need me, yet she continues to help me, teach me, and offer me a place of employment and residence. The least I can do is respect her wishes, and put all this nonsense behind me.

I took a deep breath, focusing on the world around me.

The wind was cold, yet refreshing as it brushed against my face. The shops along Front Street were quiet, though I could see customers inside the windows, browsing goods, produce, and other necessities of life.

The sound of the river rushing beneath the bridge a short ways down the road was calming, in its own way. It brought me some peace to hear its progression through the gorge that Grangehurst was built around.

I let my breath out, forcing my mind to clear.

I will forget the whole matter. There is no reason for me to dwell on it, of course. What good will it do me to think about death and violence?

I pushed the thoughts of Captain Seymour, Mrs. Morton, and Mr. Morton out of my mind, setting my thoughts instead on the few things that Lily needed.

A bottle of ink. A new pen. A fresh spool of wool from Mr. Sawyer's farm stand.

These things are much more pleasant to consider. Much more pleasant, indeed.

I set my shoulders, and took a left down Church Street, the market in the center of town visible from even where I stood.

But despite my best intentions, the shadows surrounding Grangehurst seemed to cling to me, like tendrils of smoke from a fire.

7
———

The market was as busy as it always was toward the end of the day. Vendors had restocked halfway through, expecting the influx of customers as they made their way home from work, or school, or were just preparing for their evening meals, needing to fetch a last minute ingredient.

The market stalls sat in a large, half circle, each with a different, brightly colored awning over them. The produce stall with fresh vegetables and the occasional fruits were beneath Mrs. Warren's red awning, and the green awning housed the baked goods from Mr. Clark's bakery, which was down on Front Street closer to *The Golden Spool*.

Surrounding the market stalls were some of the smaller shops that Grangehurst boasted; the florist, the confectionary, and the barber shop. The market square stood complete with a bubbling fountain in the center, with a statue of St. John, holding an olive branch, a stone dove resting on his shoulder.

I took another look at my list, seeing a few perishable items that Lily had asked me to fetch, like some eggs, as well as cream.

I made my way over to the stall with the grey awning, where Mr. Sawyer's farm stand was.

He stood behind it, rearranging a basket of apples. He looked up as I approached.

"Ah, good afternoon, Miss Dickinson," he said. He was a handsome man, with calloused hands, a pair of bright green eyes, and a greying beard that grew faster than he was able to trim it. "Pleased to see you out and about today."

"Yes, it's been some time," I said. Typically, Lily was the one who went out for the few things we would need. "Are those the last apples of the season?"

"Indeed they are," Mr. Sawyer said, laying an affectionate hand upon the basket, as if it were one of his children. "But still just as sweet as they were at first harvest."

I chewed on the inside of my lip for a moment. "Certainly tempting, though I believe Lily would be disappointed if I spent our money so frivolously."

Mr. Sawyer grinned, and I noticed he was missing a tooth further back in his mouth. "Well, how about I make you a deal? I take it your sister is in need of more wool?" he asked.

I nodded. "Yes, it's part of the reason why I'm here."

He reached down behind his stall, and a moment

later, returned with several spools of his finest wools. "If you take three spools, I'll include three apples, free of charge. I might be proud of these apples, but I also need to ensure they are taken home, where they can be enjoyed. They won't do me any good if they simply sit here in the basket and rot, now, will they?"

I smiled at him. "Oh, Mr. Sawyer," I said. "You are too kind."

He smiled as he plucked three perfect apples from the basket, and set them down beside the spools of wool. "Pick out which three you would like, and I will wrap them up for you."

"Thank you," I said. I chose the three lightest spools, knowing that Lily would appreciate those over the darker grey spools.

As he gathered my choices into a linen bag, I looked around the rather quiet square. The sun had begun to descend, and the air grew cooler with each passing moment.

I noticed Mrs. Newman near the produce, and Mrs. Clark perusing the stand that housed the books and ink bottles that I needed to stop at next.

My eyes widened and I averted my gaze, however, when I noticed the broad-shouldered figure of Captain Seymour, coming out of the barber shop directly behind Mr. Sawyer's stand.

My heart fluttered in my chest. *Why now? Why here?*

I was doing my best to try *not* to think about him, and what he might or might not have done.

Remain calm. There is no reason why he would notice you above anyone else here. He has no idea that anyone might suspect him...at least he likely doesn't yet. For now, I must keep to myself, and not make an utter fool of myself as I did last night.

I took another deep, steadying breath.

"Oh, one moment," Mr. Sawyer said, looking down at the spool in his hand. "Allow me to exchange this spool for another. The wood here is beginning to splinter, and I would not wish to send this home where you or your sister might catch one in your finger."

"Oh," I said, glancing past him to Captain Seymour, who was making his way around Mr. Sawyer's stall. *Likely on his way home. He will probably walk directly past.* "Of course. You are very thoughtful, Mr. Sawyer."

My shoulders stiffened as I continued to follow the man out of the corner of my eye. He was not on his way home as I had hoped. Instead, he seemed to be making a straight line for Mr. Sawyer's stall.

Please hurry, Mr. Sawyer. I do not wish to be here when Captain Seymour walks up to you –

"Good afternoon, Captain," Mr. Sawyer said as he straightened, his eyes falling on the tall, broad man who had just come up beside me. "I hope the day finds you well?"

I bit down so hard on the inside of my lip that the metallic taste of blood coated my tongue. *How am I to face him? Surely my expression will betray me...*

"Quite well, sir, thank you very much," Captain

Seymour said. "I am feeling a great deal more like myself now that I have had a proper shave and trim. Since leaving the military, I find myself missing the simplicities of life, including having my physique inspected by superior officers to ensure there had been adherence to the rules, one of which was to keep a closely trimmed haircut."

I glanced sideways and up at him. His dark hair indeed looked clean and refreshed, though the salt and pepper streaks just above his ears were still visible. His jawline was spotless and seemed like chiseled stone, a hard edge that was contrasted by the setting sun and the shadows beneath his chin.

He turned his gaze down to me, my attempt at discretion so easily foiled.

My eyes snapped away, fixing themselves intently upon the package that Mr. Sawyer was all too slowly putting together for me.

"Ah, Miss Dickinson," Captain Seymour said in a warm, deep voice, like the first surge of a fire's warmth in a cold fireplace. "How wonderful it is to see you."

"Likewise," I said, still not meeting his gaze, my face ablaze, cheeks burning red.

"I have been meaning to stop by *The Golden Spool* to inspect that rafter and see how it is holding up," Captain Seymour said. "I trust there have been no problems? No strange sounds or creaks?"

"N – No," I said, shaking my head like a trembling oak tree in the wind. "Everything has been perfectly fine, thank you."

"I'm pleased to hear it," he said.

Mr. Sawyer closed the bag containing my apples and the spools of wool, passing it across the market stall to me. "Here you are, Miss Dickinson. And you let your sister know that Hazel's wool has started to come back in, as black as ink. If she wishes me to save a spool or two for her, she must let me know soon, lest Mrs. Dawkins buy it all up from me."

"Of course," I said, taking the bag hastily, giving Mr. Sawyer the briefest of smiles. "I shall tell her as soon as I return home."

"Excellent," he said. He looked up at Captain Seymour. "Now, sir, what is it that I can do for you?"

That was my cue to leave. I quickly turned on my heel and started back through the market toward the other stalls at the far side of the square.

It troubled me how much I despised being in the Captain's presence. It was as if a dark cloud hung over him, or a plague rendered him entirely unapproachable.

But it is all in my own mind, isn't it? Nothing that he said or did was reprehensible, yet I treated him as if he were no better than a leper...

That didn't mean he knew I had been thinking of him that way, I realized. He might very well have been consumed with his own thoughts, and would not think anything of my behavior.

That may not be entirely true, though. Whenever I see him, I always try to be very friendly, hospitable, and kind, just as he is to Lily and me. He might find my behavior today quite strange.

I walked over to Mrs. William's stall, as I noticed she was beginning to clean up her stock for the day.

I breathed a small sigh of relief as I asked for a new bottle of ink and to see her selection of dip pens. *I can finish these last few errands and make my way back to the shop. I do not need to fret. Everything is going to be perfectly all right.*

"I'm quite fond of this kind of pen," said a voice beside me. "Though they were difficult to come by when I was in India."

I very nearly jumped out of my skin. I turned and looked up to see Captain Seymour standing there, peering over the velvet lined box of shiny pens beside me, a basket filled with apples tucked into the crook of his arm. "Oh, Captain..." I murmured. "I – I didn't see you there."

He chuckled, his face splitting into a handsome smile. "My apologies, Miss Dickinson. I did not mean to frighten you. It just appeared to me that you were having trouble selecting the right pen, so I thought I might offer my recommendation. I have signed many documents in my day, and a pen like this one has never failed me. Not once."

I swallowed hard. *I am going to have a great deal of trouble getting away from him, aren't I?*

Perhaps it wasn't all bad, however.

The only way to deal with this fear may be to face it. And in order to face it, I might need to discern the truth. It may very well be that Constable Brown will be unable to share his findings with the rest of the town for some time. Am I to suffer until then?

"I think the Captain is right," I told Mrs. Williams. "I should like the pen he recommends."

Mrs. Williams smiled and picked it out of the box to wrap up with the bottle of ink I'd chosen.

"Excellent choice," Captain Seymour said. "And when you are finished with the lady's order, I would like to purchase some stationery, please."

I debated for a moment about how to address the thoughts racing inside my mind. *Obviously, I cannot come right out and ask if he had anything to do with Mr. Morton's death, or even ask if he might have access to some foreign types of poisons.*

I stood there while Mrs. Williams prepared our orders; Mrs. Williams smiled up at the Captain as she handed him the stationery. It was likely that neither she nor Mr. Sawyer had heard the newest rumors from Mrs. Minford yet, which was good. Otherwise, they might have treated him the same way I had.

Perhaps it is best to treat him as innocent until he is proven to be otherwise. And above all, I still have a difficult time believing that he might have been the attacker.

"Are you on your way back to the shop?" Captain Seymour asked as he slid the bundle of stationery beneath his other arm.

I took the package from Mrs. Williams with a smile before looking up at him. "I am, yes."

"Then allow me to walk that way with you," he said.

I debated for only a moment. *This could be the chance I need to set my mind at ease.*

"Very well," I replied.

"Good," he said. "And would you allow me to carry your purchases for you?"

"Oh, it's quite all right – " I said, but before the words had escaped me, he had managed to gingerly remove the boxes and packages from my arms.

He smiled at me, looking toward the road, his arms now fully laden with goods. "Shall we?"

I fell into step beside him, the coolness of the day passing over me as we started down Church Street together.

"There has been a buzz in the air today," Captain Seymour said. "I'm certain it has to do with what happened to the unfortunate Mr. Morton last night."

The color returned to my face, and I gaped at the ground at my feet.

It shouldn't be such a shock that he mentioned it, as it seemed to be the topic of conversation on almost everyone's lips, but to hear it from the man who might have been involved in the whole business? It seemed... out of place. Almost like an admission.

"I have heard of little else today..." I said, realizing that it was best to appear as yet another concerned citizen, knowing as little as everyone else. "It seemed to be all anyone could talk about in the shop today."

"Yes, indeed," he said. "Poor fellow…dropping dead in the middle of the street the way he did."

His gaze was fixed on the horizon, and concern creased his straight brows, wrinkling his broad forehead. "I have seen a great many deaths in my life…far too many, if I am honest. No man should have to endure the sorts of sights I have witnessed…" he said in a low voice as we came to the intersection of Church and Front Streets. "But it is something quite different to witness it on a battlefield, in the line of duty, rather than to learn about it happening to a man who lives in your own hometown. One expects the places where we live to be immune to such tragedies, so it is the place that I believe we feel them the deepest."

I studied him carefully. Genuine concern was reflected in his eyes as he looked down at me. Surely that was not the sort of emotion one could pretend? Compassion and concern could not be imitated. And his eyes were clear, without any trouble meeting my own.

"I cannot imagine the sort of tragedies that you have witnessed," I said. "It must be difficult to try and live out an ordinary life, having to push those sorts of memories aside."

"Too true," he said. "But one learns to appreciate life a little more when faced with death so frequently. What else is there to do? It would be easy enough to wallow in sorrow, I suppose, and waste the time we have been so graciously given. Or, we can look for joy and hope, for they do exist, and choose to focus on them instead. I find life much more pleasant when I am able to remain focused on what is good in the world around me."

Admirable, for certain. But is this simply to divert suspicion away from himself?

I reprimanded myself.

Why would he feel the need to divert suspicion when speaking to me? I am no one, apart from the spinster who works in the dress shop across the street from his home. Besides, the information he shares with me is unprompted. Why share his heart like this unless he meant it?

"Has it been difficult to adjust again to life in England since returning from India?" I asked. "I imagine things are quite different. The food, the way of life, the access to certain goods…"

I belatedly realized that asking about the goods might give me away, but it was too late to take back my words.

"I certainly learned the culture while living there," Captain Seymour said, adjusting some of the packages in his arms. They seemed more cumbersome than heavy, as if he carried a pile of feathered pillows instead of apples and paper. "But in my heart, I always longed for England. I missed the cool evenings, the rolling hills, the rain…and I missed Grangehurst. India was exciting, certainly, and yes, I had access to foods and other things that I could never dream of here…"

My heart skipped a beat. Could that mean –

"Yet, there is very little I felt the need to bring home with me from India," he said. "A few mementos, some clothing, and gifts that were bestowed upon me. When I came back to England, I wanted my home to feel properly English, not as if I had brought India back with me. I will cherish the memories I have from my time there, but that is where they need to remain; there."

"I understand," I said with a nod.

We stopped just outside *The Golden Spool,* and he smiled down at me. "Well, here you are, Miss Dickinson. Thank you for your company on our way home. I apologize if my conversation became morose. I shall endeavor to tell you stories of my adventures the next time we speak. Perhaps you should like to hear about the time I had to ride an elephant when I missed the train I had intended to travel in?"

Unbidden, a smile spread across my face at the thought. "An elephant, Captain?"

He grinned, the worry fading from his face. "Indeed. How could I possibly make something like that up?"

"I suppose you could not," I said, perhaps with a bit more weight than I'd meant to.

8
———

The Captain passed me the packages I had purchased before heading across the street to his own home. I watched him leave.

It wasn't the Captain. It couldn't possibly have been him...could it?

Why I so badly wanted to believe that, I could not be sure. Some sort of feeling deep in my soul. The way he spoke of death, and his regret of it...or perhaps it was his concern for Mr. Morton. I didn't want to believe such kindness could be false.

Regardless, I did not see Lily when I stepped back inside the shop a few moments later.

"You're back already?"

I found her standing at the back of the shop, which was currently empty apart from the two of us. She had Miss Baldwin's dress draped over one of her mannequins and was working on some of the lace details on the train.

"Yes," I said, setting the packages down on the front counter. "I purchased everything you needed."

"That's good," she said, still deftly moving the needle in and out of the lace as she looked up at me. "But I thought you were to take a long walk, clear your thoughts."

"Yes, well…" I said. "The thoughts seemed to follow me, regardless of whether or not I wanted to be free of them."

Lily's gaze hardened. "Iris, I told you that you must let go this entire matter."

"And I had every intention of doing so," I said, staring back at her in exasperation. "But what was I to do when Captain Seymour appeared in the market at the same time I did, and needed to shop at the same stalls I did?"

Lily rolled her eyes, abandoning the stitching for a moment to turn and glare at me. "Surely you could have ignored him and focused on something else? I imagine he was not the only person at the market?"

"Of course," I said. "But it was quite difficult when he wanted to speak with me, and then to discuss Mr. Morton, just like everyone else in town seems to want to do."

Lily huffed, shaking her head. "Why is it that everyone can think of nothing else?" she asked, returning to the dress. "It is the most ridiculous nonsense, expelling one's energies on hypothesizing about how the man met his demise. It is gruesome."

"But you must realize that this is the first tragedy

our town has experienced in quite some time," I said. "You cannot expect everyone to remain silent."

Lily's skilled hands paused, and she looked back up at me. "What do you mean?" she asked. I realized some of the color had drained from her face, though I could see no reason for the sudden change in her demeanor.

My eyes narrowed. "I am saying that when a tragedy like this happens in a small town such as Grangehurst, people tend to feel it deeply," I said. "One doesn't ever expect these sorts of disasters to happen near their own home."

Lily studied my face for a long, hard moment. "That is the truth…" she admitted, slowly looking back to the dress.

"It's what Captain Seymour said," I told her. "I cannot take the words for my own."

"I see," Lily said. "Well…I suppose that makes sense, then. A man with his background would surely be disturbed if something as terrible as what he experienced in the military had somehow followed him home."

I pursed my lips. "You have such logical sense, sister," I said. "You never cease to astound me."

She looked away, as if unsure how to respond.

"He didn't do it," I said, shaking my head. "The Captain, I mean. I'm almost certain of it."

"How?" Lily asked with a note of sarcasm. "Did you ask him?"

"Of course not," I said, frowning at her.

"I'm pleased to hear it," she said. "Can you imagine what he would think of us if you had?"

"I have more sense than that," I said, unpacking the box containing the ink and pen. "But if you had heard the way he spoke of death, of the way he had chosen to focus on the good, and the hope that can be found around us…you would agree with me."

"Perhaps I would," Lily said.

"Does it not distress you that an innocent man could be accused of murder?" I asked.

"By whom?" Lily asked pointedly. "You?"

My face flooded with color. "I – no," I said. "If Mrs. Minford suspects it, then it likely will be all over town before the end of the day. Then the Constable will catch wind of it and then he will surely investigate."

"Unless he sees no merit in it," Lily said, picking up an extra piece of lace from the shelf beside her, beginning to unravel it. "Iris, you must realize that there are people who are much more skilled in these matters than you. They will take the necessary precautions, and they will not allow the guilty to escape justice. You need to trust that."

"I do trust the Constable," I said. "But he seemed troubled by the whole matter, and then to learn that Mr. Morton had been poisoned? This seems to be a great deal more than a crime of passion, doesn't it?"

"Crime of passion?" Lily asked.

"I've read about them in my novels," I said, somewhat sourly. "Those sorts of murders that happen spur of the moment, when someone flies into a rage out of a deep, emotional hurt – "

"I'm quite familiar with what they are," Lily said, her eyes narrowed.

She set the lace back down, and walked over to me. She folded her arms in front of herself, and stared at me, her gaze intense, holding me in place.

"Why are you so determined to prove his innocence?" she asked. "You do realize that the more involved you become, the greater the possibility of attracting scandal. We shouldn't be associated with such a sordid business."

I considered it for a long, hard moment.

Why was I so determined?

Perhaps more than any other reason, because I was frightened. I didn't think I could bear the thought of someone like the Captain being involved, but if not him, then it had to be *someone* else in town, didn't it?

And how would I be able to bear that reality any more?

"The idea of someone capable of murder...of taking the life of another human being...is just too much to bear. But if that man were to be living across the street from us?" I asked.

Lily's face suddenly became difficult to read, which at once told me how deep in thought she truly was.

She walked around behind the counter, pulling the apples from the bag where her woolen spools were residing.

"What is it?" I asked. "You have become awfully silent."

She looked up. "I must admit, your point is valid, and one I had not considered..." she said. "If the Captain was indeed the reason for Mr. Morton's death, then everyone will know it. Not only will they know it, but they will do everything they can to avoid his home after that. If they avoid his home, then they will likely avoid any of the shops nearby, as well. And we are directly across the street."

She frowned. "I don't like this," she continued. "Any of it. I want to keep our distance from this matter. That would be best, of course. Keeping our hands clean, our reputations unsullied...However, I realize that our very nearness to where Mr. Morton passed away may be enough to keep us firmly planted in the rumors surrounding his death while we wait for the Constable to learn the truth. And even then, how can we be certain there won't be those who would question our innocence?"

"You're saying that some people might accuse...us?" I asked, stunned.

"Us, or the Captain, given our proximity," she said. "Though the Captain certainly seems to be the more obvious choice, given his history in the military, but also his ties to India and whatever sort of goods he might have brought back to England with him."

My heart fluttered in my chest. "I hadn't considered that in some peoples' minds we might become entangled in it all..."

Lily nodded. "For these reasons, I believe it might be in our best interests to find the truth," she said. "I, for one, would be relieved to know that we are not, in fact, living next door to a murderer."

"You're changing your mind?" I asked.

"Not exactly," Lily said. "I am simply saying that we might have to learn the truth about what happened. Think of Mrs. Minford. She thought nothing of accusing the Captain of being the one to poison Mr. Morton, which may be the furthest possibility from the truth. But in her mind, it made sense, given his tie to foreign people and places. What might prevent her from inventing such rumors about us as well?"

I pursed my lips. "She wouldn't spread rumors about us," I said. "We do business with her, and she has always been kind to us."

"But if we are associated by proximity with this newest scandal, then her attitude might quickly change," Lily said. "No. It's best if we nip this in the bud as soon as possible."

I took a shuddering breath, my stomach twisting into knots. I hadn't wanted to be involved in this ordeal, yet here was Lily, agreeing to pry into it.

Does she believe in the Captain's innocence as well? Or is she looking to prove him guilty?

"One thing is for certain..." my sister said with a firm expression. "Our involvement must be from a discreet distance, of course. It will not do to reveal our intentions."

"Agreed," I said.

She looked up at me, her brow furrowing. "I thought this was what you wanted?" she asked.

I said, "I am not certain what I wanted. I want Captain Seymour to be innocent. I want the guilty to be found, but on the other hand, I am quite terrified about *who* it might end up being. What if it's someone else we know?"

"Oh, it will very likely be someone we know," Lily said in a flat tone that was not very reassuring. "We must be brave, dear sister. Darkness has settled over Grangehurst, and I fear we have only seen the beginning of it."

9

I still found it rather strange that Lily had agreed to help me discover the truth about what happened to Mr. Morton. The more I considered it, however, the more I realized that I didn't want to discern who had committed the crime, precisely, as much as I wanted to find a way to prove Captain Seymour's innocence.

The following morning, a pleasant and mild Friday, I found myself feeling a great deal better about everything. A good night's sleep had helped to clear my thoughts, and had given me a much more positive outlook on all that had been happening in our lives.

The sunlight seemed to lift our spirits, as well. Lily even hummed to herself as she sliced up one of the apples that Mr. Sawyer had sent home with me the day before.

"These are the last of his harvest?" Lily asked,

setting another slice into the bowl resting beside her on the table.

"Yes," I said as I spread fresh jam over the bread I had just cut. "He said he didn't want them to rot."

Lily considered the last half of the apple. "Perhaps I shall make a pie with the other two," she said.

My eyes widened. "Or what of that applesauce our mother used to make?" I asked. "With the cinnamon sweets?"

Lily looked over at me, and a sad smile spread across her face. "You remember Mother's applesauce?"

I looked away, suddenly sheepish. "I know I don't remember a great deal, but I do remember that applesauce. It was pink, wasn't it? I always found the color perfectly lovely."

"Yes…" Lily said, staring down at the apple in her hand with renewed affection. "I found it lovely, too."

Resolving to do exactly that, we ate our breakfast and made our way down to the shop just before it was to open.

As soon as Lily tied her apron around her waist, she flipped open the order book. "Now, we have Mrs. Newman's daughters' dresses to work on, of course. How are they coming?"

"I have the eldest daughter's finished," I said, checking the neatly stacked garments in the shelves behind the counter, where we kept orders to be picked up. "And the second eldest's will be finished as soon as I sew the buttons into the back."

"Very good," Lily said. "I shall be finishing the

floral details on Miss Baldwin's wedding gown this morning, and – "

A low knock reverberated from the front door of the shop.

Lily and I both looked over, and found Captain Seymour peering inside, waving at us.

My stomach twisted into nervous knots, and I glanced over at Lily.

"I suppose it is only a few minutes before we open," Lily said, setting down the veil that was meant to match Miss Baldwin's dress. She made her way over to the door, which she had yet to unlock.

As she did, I noticed the stiffness in her shoulders. She was a great deal more nervous about speaking with him than she had let me know.

"Good morning, Captain," Lily said, staring up at the man. He nearly took up the entire doorframe. "Is there something I can help you with?" she asked.

"I was hoping that I might speak with you and your sister, if you have a moment," he said. "I realize that your days become busy very quickly, and I do not wish to take up more of your time than necessary."

Lily glanced over her shoulder at me, some of the color missing from her face, her mouth a hard line. "I suppose we have a few moments before anyone is likely to arrive," she said, pulling the door open, and standing aside.

Captain Seymour smiled warmly at her, and ducked as he stepped inside.

His eyes fell on me near the counter, and he waved. "Good morning, Miss Iris. How are you?"

"Well, Captain," I said. "And you?"

"I am doing quite well, thank you," he said.

He pulled his hat from his head, running his fingers through his dark hair, though it hardly needed smoothing, short as it was.

"What can we do for you, Captain?" Lily asked, coming to stand beside me.

"My request is quite simple," he said. "As I am sure you ladies know, I have not been back in Grangehurst for long. It has taken me some weeks to settle back into the ways of life here in England, and I am very appreciative of the company I have received, from the both of you, as well as from others in town. However, I feel a great deal has changed since I lived here over twenty years ago. Naturally, of course, but even still, I find myself a stranger in my own town."

"I imagine that has been difficult," Lily said in a matter-of-fact tone.

"Indeed," the Captain said. "I hope to remedy this by throwing a dinner party at my home. I should like to invite as many people in town as I can, as a way of introducing myself to them, and getting to know everyone once again."

Lily glanced over at me.

"I think it's a wonderful idea," I said, and genuinely thought it was. "I imagine many will be quite pleased to have the chance to get to know you, or to reacquaint themselves with you."

"I agree," Lily said. "I'm sure there will be many who have questions about your time in India, as well as your service in the military."

"It will be a wonderful opportunity for me to answer those questions and more," he said. "I also hope to familiarize myself with all the faces I pass by on a daily basis. I have never been much good with names, but I hope by making friends with those who attend, I shall be able to feel more at home here once again."

I glanced at Lily, feeling her gaze on my face.

I was certain there was a sort of language that only siblings could decipher, and each family had their own unique way of speaking to one another without words. Lily may have been nearly ten years my senior, but that didn't prevent us from creating glances and arches of the brow to communicate with one another from across the shop, conveying discomfort or annoyance, or even perhaps surprise. She had mastered, however, the sort of look to cause my knees to shake beneath my skirts out of fear. I couldn't remember what sort of discipline our mother might have used with us when we were young girls, but I imagined that Lily's leveling glances might have been of the same sort.

For the moment, in that brief glance we shared, I realized just how uncomfortable she was about the matter at hand. A dinner party was one thing, but for it to be given by a man whom we suspected could very well be a murderer...

No. He isn't a murderer. Perhaps this will be the perfect opportunity to prove that once and for all.

"Are we the first you have invited?" Lily asked, folding her arms, her eyes narrowing ever so slightly.

The Captain, despite his size, suddenly became rather sheepish. "Well...yes. In fact, you are. I might say that it was merely convenience that brought me here first, as you both live directly across the street from my own home, but that wouldn't be the entire truth. No, I had hoped that you two might be able to point me in the direction of those who would be interested in attending, as well as those whom I might avoid. I realize my return to Grangehurst may not be seen as welcome, as I've heard from some that when I left, I abandoned the place I called home. And in my long absence, they further solidified that belief."

"That seems rather unfair," Lily said, though I detected a note of reluctance in her voice. I could see the hesitation in her gaze, the calculated decision that she weighed carefully as she watched him.

I swallowed hard, thinking about how I, myself, perceived the situation at hand. Certainly the Captain was in need, but it was for such a small matter... Yet he behaved as though it were a matter of life and death.

Perhaps it is, in a way...the life or death of his social acceptance here in Grangehurst.

The people of Grangehurst were kind and reasonable. I could easily say so, having known them for the entirety of my life. I may not have remembered much from when I was young, but I could still recall glimpses of the people that I saw on a frequent basis; the scent of the freshly baking bread in the bakery, the sound of horse hooves clattering down the streets, the sound of the river down in the gorge, swelling with the winter snow melt and ebbing with the heat of the summer.

We were all quite familiar with one another. We helped and cared for one another.

That said, our neighbors were set in their ways. Many believed the country to be changing so quickly, so drastically, that it was sure to be of detriment to us all. They preferred instead for everything to remain as it had always been.

The Captain's reappearance, and from spending so many years in India, no less, had been nothing short of the most talked about occurrence I could recall in some time. It seemed his name was on everyone's lips, and I was certain that most of it was not to be regarded as positive or encouraging conversation.

"What of Mrs. Minford?" Lily asked, her brow furrowing once more. "Surely she would be able to point you in the right direction."

I gaped at her. Mrs. Minford? Was she joking?

The Captain grinned, surprisingly, though it was clear from his averted gaze that he was rather embarrassed. "I…considered it," he said slowly. "However, I remember Mrs. Minford quite well as a younger woman, and she was as much of a busybody then as she is now. I fear that if I was to go to her, I might be setting myself up for…well, a great deal more scrutiny than I am prepared to handle."

I looked over at my sister, wishing for her to know how much I agreed with his assessment, but she refused to meet my gaze.

Lily, to my great astonishment, returned his smile with one of her own. "I am pleased to see that you do remember Grangehurst, Captain Seymour."

Was she testing him?

That seemed strange to me, but how was I to know the depths of my sister's mind?

"Very well," Lily said. "We shall come to your aid, if only to help you avoid scrutiny by Mrs. Minford. She should be at the top of your list, however. If you do not invite her, she will make sure you are aware of her displeasure, along with every other living creature in this town."

"Of course," he said. "I simply did not wish to tie myself to her. I realize that one must be wise when it comes to who they share information with…especially personal information."

"Quite right," Lily said.

She and I proceeded to give him a short list of those he might benefit by inviting. Most notably, we told him to invite most of the shop owners, the mayor, the fire chief, the constable, and the pub owner.

"These are the people in town with the most influence," Lily said. "They will be the best to connect with, especially if you have any questions about the current state of affairs within Grangehurst."

"Thank you," the Captain said, relief clear on his face. Dimples appeared in the corners of his mouth, giving him an almost youthful appearance. "I recognize a few of these names...but I am certain it will do me good to reacquaint myself with them, as well as meet the newer residents."

"Very few of these people are new," Lily said. "Perhaps they are simply the children of those you knew, or the new owners when the shops changed hands over the years."

I watched Lily carefully, wondering why on earth she was being so agreeable. She had made it perfectly clear that she wanted nothing more than to keep her distance from this whole situation, yet here she was, investing in him and his connections to the town.

What are you up to, Lily?

"I really must thank you ladies again," the Captain said, sliding the list inside the pocket of his coat. "This has been a tremendous help to me."

"You are quite welcome," Lily said.

"Indeed," I said.

"I must now insist that I compensate you in some way," he said, looking about. "Here you are, taking time out of your morning as you prepare for the day, and I have certainly taken up too much of it."

"You need not repay us in any way," Lily said, shaking her head.

"Then how about a favor?" the Captain asked. "Sometime in the future, if you need anything...*anything* at all...you let me know, and I shall be of service."

A smile stretched across Lily's face. "I suppose there is no harm in that, is there?"

"Certainly not," the Captain said. "Well, I must be off. I now have personal invitations to deliver – Oh!" he exclaimed, turning from the door he had walked to. "Dinner will be served at eight, so please feel free to stop over whenever is agreeable to you before then."

"Wonderful," Lily said.

"Thank you again for the invitation," I said. "It is very kind of you."

He smiled, tipping his hat to us. "It is my pleasure. Truly. Have a splendid day, ladies, and I shall see you tomorrow evening."

With that, he pulled open the door and ducked back outside.

As soon as the door had closed smartly behind him, Lily spun away, heading back toward the trio of mirrors and the mannequin that held Miss Baldwin's dress.

"That was all…surprising," I said, following after her.

"Hardly," she said, sparing me just a glance as she pulled her box of satins and silks from behind the mirrors. "It's perfectly reasonable that a man such as he would throw a dinner party like this. It's customary when moving to a new place, even if he lived here years before."

"No," I said, watching as she pulled a spool of thread so fine that we had taken to calling it "spider's silk" from the box, its sheen glimmering in the sunlight streaming through the back window. "I mean your response to him."

She stood straight, turning to regard me with confusion. "What do you mean?"

"Being so willing to help him, so friendly," I said, shaking my head in disbelief. "I thought you were determined to stay out of all this."

She sighed, shaking her head. "Dear Iris, surely you could see why?" she asked. "By agreeing to help, and agreeing to attend this dinner party of his, we have given ourselves an opportunity to find proof, one way or another, as to his involvement in Mr. Morton's death."

I blinked at her. "Sister, you were being devious?"

Lily's brow furrowed. "Devious? I think not. Resourceful, perhaps. You see, we have now earned his trust, so when we inevitably sneak off to look through his home for any signs of – "

"*Lily,*" I said, scathingly. "You *cannot* be serious! Sneaking off? Have you lost your senses?"

"Certainly not," Lily said.

"And why do you suddenly care so much about finding the proof?" I asked. "You were utterly determined to keep our distance."

"Of course I am," Lily said. "But sometimes that will have to be nothing more than in a metaphorical sense. He must not know we suspect him."

My mind raced with thoughts and questions.

"Did you hear nothing of what I said the last time we spoke of this?" Lily asked. "We must look into it, if only to maintain and preserve our own reputations. And the sooner we can attend to these matters, the sooner we can set aside any possible suspicion that could be laid at our doorstep."

I asked, "You are truly so frightened of what others in town might think of us? Surely you cannot believe they would suspect *our* involvement, we've never done a thing to garner such disapproving – "

"My dear Iris," Lily interrupted firmly. "You are ten years my junior, and while I realize that you have seen your fair share of this world, I do believe there is still a great deal you must learn."

I found my heart jolting at her words, a heated anger passing through my veins but for a moment. "What do you mean, precisely, dear sister?" I asked, not caring to hide the edge in my words.

"I mean no harm," Lily said, though in as unfeeling a way as possible. "Only that in my time, I have seen that a person's good opinion of someone else can be as easily lost in response to a rumor or a curt word as anything. I believe it is far easier to think less of a man or woman than to respect him or her."

I pursed my lips. "I...suppose you are right," I said.

A cloud passed over the sun outside, sending the interior of the shop into deeper shadow. That made it difficult to see my sister's face, so far from the windows as she was.

The clock on the top of the shelf that held the spools of fabrics chimed, drawing my gaze, breaking the tense silence between Lily and me. It was nearly eight.

I sighed, making my way over to the front door, checking to make sure that the sign hanging in the window had been switched from *Closed* to *Open*. It indeed had.

"Well..." I said, peering out into the street. It seemed that the other shops had begun to open their doors, and townsfolk streamed in and out of them, going about the first duties of their days.

"Well, what?" Lily asked, somewhat crossly. It seemed she didn't take kindly to my bout of anger. "Out with it. You know how I dislike your trailing sentences."

I bit down on the end of my tongue. It would do us no good to argue before the start of our day. If anything, it was sure to make the hours long and unendurable.

I turned, realizing we had but moments to clear the air before the first of our customers were sure to arrive. "Well, then what are we to do?" I asked. "Should we go to the Constable once again?"

"For what reason?" Lily asked, straightening the box of lace with the tip of her shoe, pushing it back beneath the table where we cut and trimmed fabrics. "We have learned nothing new."

"No, but what of the dinner?" I asked. "Would it not be prudent for us to inform him that the Captain is hosting this party? So that he may keep an eye on him?"

"Do not be ridiculous, Iris," Lily said. "Hosting a dinner party is no crime. No, we should discern whether or not there is anything about the Captain to share in the first place. Which is why this dinner shall prove to be such a great opportunity."

I hoped this would be of greater advantage to us than what it seemed to be at the moment. I worried that we were seeing what was not there, and that we might be suspecting someone needlessly. What then? What if he were to find out that we doubted him?

"Still…we must appear distant," Lily said, with a firm nod. "If we are caught looking into the matter, regardless of whether or not it was of our own volition, then we are sure to draw attention that we do not want or need."

"Of course," I said, after a moment's reflection. That seemed reasonable, and I was determined to see reason in regards to the situation. "That makes the most sense."

"Good," Lily said, the matter settled. "Now hand me the smaller scissors, if you please. I am nearly a quarter of an hour behind schedule, and I do not wish to delay my work any longer."

10

"What do you think of this dress?"

I looked up from my vanity table to see Lily standing in the doorway. My eyes widened as they looked upon a drab, tired looking dress in a slate grey. It hung loosely on my sister's already delicate, thin frame, but drained her face of what little color it had, and made her usually pretty dark hair look more like spilled ink than the silky raven's feathers I usually compared it to in my thoughts.

I opened my mouth for a brief moment before promptly closing it once again.

"What?" Lily asked, her already severe expression becoming even more so. "Why are you looking at me like that?"

I certainly loved my dear sister, but she had a difficult time finding her way around the more social events of life. She would never admit to it, of course, and if I presented the fact to her, she would dismiss it as useless and unproductive knowledge, despite standing before me and asking for my help.

What surprised me more, however, was her ability to create, with such great detail, dresses of elegance, all of them perfect for the clients they were made for, and yet be unable to choose something for herself.

"I...well," I said, unsure how to proceed.

I glanced between her and the door to the armoire we shared, just within sight through the doorway to the bedroom, where Lily stood. I hesitated for only a moment before leaping up and hurrying past her, my eyes fixed on the armoire door.

"What is it?" Lily asked, clearly growing impatient with me. "Why are you – "

"Try this instead," I said, pulling the door open and reaching for a deep, emerald green dress from the back of the rod upon which it hung. I turned around, the fabric of the dress swirling as I proffered it to her. "It will suit your eyes best."

Lily accepted the dress in my outstretched hand, though her expression was cool. I had not admitted her dress choice to be poor, but I may as well have, offering her an alternative.

Neither was she gracious enough to thank me for it, as she turned and made her way back to the bedroom without a word.

I suppose her pride and my desire to be honest with her will always be at odds.

Just as I finished pinning the last stray curl of

blonde hair into the chignon I so fancied, the door to the bedroom swung outward once more, and Lily stepped out into our sitting room.

I smiled at her. "Oh, Lily... Have a look at yourself."

I jumped up from the stool and took her arm, leading her to the floor-length mirror that leaned against the wall.

"Well, certainly you look elegant," Lily said, her nose wrinkling slightly as she stared at our reflections. "You always do."

"I think you look perfectly lovely in that dress," I said. "It's one you made, may I remind you."

"Yes, I am well aware," she said, picking at the matching green lace at the elbow. "And my technique has drastically improved within the last few years."

"Oh, do not frown at yourself so much," I said, squeezing her arm. "You will fit right in at this party."

"I certainly hope so," Lily said, giving her dark hair a small fluff with the tips of her fingers. "The last thing we need to do is stand out this evening."

"Oh...right," I said. "I very nearly forgot why we were going to this dinner in the first place."

Lily turned, giving me a flat look. "We must remain vigilant this evening. No one is to know of our suspicions. If anyone brings up Mr. Morton's murder, as they undoubtedly will – "

"It will very likely be Mrs. Minford, of course," I said.

"Quite right," Lily said, tugging at the ends of her sleeves. "Regardless, we must appear as uninformed as everyone else. Even less so, if we can manage it. You, therefore, my affectionate sister, must do your best to mask your thoughts which appear so easily in your expressions."

"Yes. I shall do my best," I said, knowing that she knew my habits well, perhaps even better than I did.

After she allowed me to arrange her hair, which she kept fussing with, we made our way downstairs and out into the twilight that had fallen over Grangehurst.

The Captain's house across the street was in many ways quite similar to ours. It was a part of the row of shops and homes that lined the main street in town, with only the façade of each building indicating the distinct differences between the homes and shops. While ours was simple, built of brick, the frames painted in white, the Captain's residence was constructed of stone, much like the shops on either side. The upper stories were white washed plaster, with large windows set into the walls, each of which allowed the light from inside to pour out into the night.

"It seems the Captain was able to garner quite a few guests," Lily said as we approached the front door, which stood open.

I concurred, as I stared through to the rather grand foyer, where nearly a dozen people were gathered, many of whom were staring around.

I suppressed a shiver as we approached the door, the realization that we might be stepping into the home of a murderer washing over me. *There is no proof yet. He may very well be innocent.*

I knew I had to keep my mind clear, lest I fall into the temptation of suspecting him more than I already did. I needed to be as objective as possible, and I realized how difficult that was proving to be.

We stepped up to the front door, the two of us exchanging a glance; mine nervous, Lily's determined. She nodded at me and walked through the doorway into the house.

Light washed over us, warm and inviting, and a heady scent of burning incense wafted from some unseen source. It was nothing compared to the decorations in the foyer, however, which was lavishly done and rather crowded. And not just with people.

The walls were covered with paintings, each of them beautiful and colorful. My eye was drawn to a large portrait of an elephant adorned with bright blue and yellow silks, golden tassels hanging from behind its ears and over its forehead. Another showed an exotic city, the roofline painted in the rubies and golds of sunset. These paintings had been placed on the wall so close together that it was almost impossible to see the polished wood of the paneling beneath.

They weren't the only impressive parts of the room. Gilded tables stood along the walls, filled with artifacts and instruments of unknown origins. Vases of blown glass and statues of marble were positioned between carved chairs and tall, sweeping fronds of plants. It seemed the Captain had been less than honest when he had claimed to bring very little back with him from his travels.

"My, his taste in décor is quite...eclectic," Lily whispered.

"I'm having a difficult time knowing where exactly I should look," I murmured in return. "Can we be certain there is any more to his home? I cannot even see another doorway – "

"Ah, good evening, ladies."

We turned as if of one mind to the voice that had spoken to us from somewhere beside an impressive palm frond protruding from a blue glazed pot.

My eyes swept over the cluttered space before falling upon Captain Seymour, who was seated beside the door in one of his carved chairs.

"Ah, good evening, Captain," Lily said with a tight smile.

Captain Seymour stood, and it was at that moment that I noticed the military garb he had chosen to wear. His coat was of deepest red, like a glass of fine wine, and medals and pins gleamed in the candlelight upon his chest, all of which he proudly displayed.

"You ladies look lovely, the both of you," Captain Seymour said, smiling at each of us in turn. "Miss Lily, that dress is quite becoming. It makes your eyes shine."

Lily's face flushed ever so slightly, though I imagined it was difficult for the Captain to see in the low light. "Thank you, Captain. I see that your party has had quite the turn out?"

"I suppose it has," Captain Seymour said, glancing

at the crowd of guests at the far side of the foyer. "Yes, I just finished informing them that dinner will be served in…" He glanced down and pulled a golden pocket watch from the inside of his jacket. "Ah, yes. In ten minutes. I have asked them all to wait, just as I will ask you."

"Very well," Lily said. "I must say, Captain, your home is furnished in a very exciting manner."

"Do you think so?" he asked, looking around with a smile tugging at the corner of his lips. "I should like to tell you the story of each and every piece, but I fear we would be here until Christmas, for certain."

"I imagine they are souvenirs from your time in India?" I asked, glancing up at the painting of the elephant.

"Indeed they are," the Captain said with a proud smile. "They took me many years to collect, and a great fortune to bring them all back to Grangehurst."

"I imagine it did," Lily said. I heard how little impressed she was in her tone.

There was a sound of excitement, and I looked over to see Mrs. Minford hurrying toward us. "Ladies! Oh, how pleased I am that you are here," she said. She took each of us by the hand, squeezing tightly. "I just knew that he might have invited you, and how glad I am that he did. Now I will not be alone."

Lily glanced past her. "Yet I see both your husband and your sister," she pointed out.

"Oh, yes, yes," the older lady said with a dismissive wave. "They are all well and fine, but if I want to have *civil* conversation, then I know that I can count on the both of you. What do you think of this home? I have not yet had the pleasure of being here, and I certainly find it to be…well, rather *interesting,* is it not?"

I could only imagine what she intended to share with anyone who might listen about just how *interesting* Captain Seymour's home was.

"I admit, I have never seen so many paintings in all my life," she continued. "Nor such intricate rugs. Upon my word, I told Mr. Minford that he must send for an Indian rug for our drawing room. I insisted that he find the same buyer that Captain Seymour has used. I desire something as exotic and exquisite."

"It is remarkable, indeed," I said. "And what of – "

The creaking of a door opening drew our attention away from our conversation. From a hidden part along the wall, a servant in a dark suit stepped through a secret door. "Sir? Your meal awaits."

"Wonderful," Captain Seymour said, clapping his hands together, making his way toward the door. "Ladies and gentlemen, if you would please follow me, we may begin our dinner."

I glanced sidelong at Lily. Suddenly, the prospect of finding evidence as to whether or not the Captain had something to do with Mr. Morton's murder seemed almost impossible. How were we to discern anything with so many guests around? Were we to question the Captain? Were we meant to stumble upon something in his home that would give us the answers we were hoping for?

"Are you all right?" Lily asked, her brow furrowing slightly.

"...Yes," I said. "Perfectly."

We followed the rest of the crowd through the door into a room that caused many of those before us to let out various forms of exclamation.

"Have you seen the chandelier?"

"Oh, good heavens, look at the table!"

"What of those chairs? And the china!"

It was easy to see what astounded them as soon as we entered. Where I had expected a lavish, elegant space, I found myself staring at something entirely exotic.

The table seemed to be the trunk of a tree cut in half, sanded down, and laid outstretched across the length of the room. It was polished so finely that the chandelier hanging overhead, which was made from half a dozen lanterns hanging at varying lengths, was nearly perfectly reflected in its surface.

The chairs that surrounded the table were lined with animal hide, and each seemed to be made from a different type of wood. A rug, as beautiful and intricate as the one in the foyer, was stretched beneath the table.

"You'll find your names on small place cards on the plates," Captain Seymour said, a gleam in his eye as he peered around Lily and I who were at the back of the group. "Please, make yourselves comfortable, and my servants will be around to offer you some refreshments."

I followed Lily, who seemed just as indifferent to

her surroundings as she had in the foyer. I knew her well enough, though, to catch her glancing toward the far wall where heads of strange creatures had been mounted on the stone wall above the fireplace, or toward the windows that looked out over the street toward our shop, framed in drapes of silk surely brought home from India.

If I know my sister at all, she will ask him about the fabric of the drapes before the night is out, and whether or not he still has any that she may use. Perhaps he would have enough for the head of a pin cushion? Or a handkerchief?

It was hard to imagine, however, that she would wish to borrow anything from a man who might, in fact, be a murderer.

"Come now, Miss Iris! Why the long face? Surely you cannot be displeased with my dinner party so soon?"

I turned to see the Captain watching me quite closely with a scrutinizing gaze.

"Oh, no, of course not, Captain," I said as casually as I could. "I am simply overcome by the splendor, and have yet to decide which aspects of your magnificent home I like best."

He beamed at me. "Wonderful. I hope you will hold off on making your decision until you have seen the rest of my home. I believe you and your sister will particularly like what I have done with the parlor, given the sheer amount of cotton and silk I acquired to accomplish it."

Perhaps he knows us better than I imagined.

Lily and I found our places toward the far end of the table, only two or three down from the head where the Captain planted himself. He smiled warmly at all of the guests down the long table, which, after a quick count, I realized sat nearly two dozen people.

I recognized many of the people that Lily and I had suggested he invite, as well as a few others who we ought to have. Mrs. Minford, of course, sat across the table from Lily and me, and had already begun to dominate the conversation, as she always did. I gave Mrs. Baldwin, the mother of the bride-to-be, a small wave as she noticed me, and overheard Lily's greeting to Mr. Clark, the baker, and his wife beside him.

All in all, it was quite a cheery gathering, and I soon found myself at ease as a servant came around the table, offering a wassail that was the Captain's own grandmother's personal recipe.

"Delicious," Lily said, eyeing the cup in her hand. "Surprisingly so."

"Oh, this is just wonderful," Mrs. Minford said, her voice carrying across the table. She giggled, showing the cup in her hand to her husband. "This reminds me of a punch that my father used to make every Sunday. It was just as tart, and lingered on the tongue just as long, which is always ideal in a punch such as this."

"I'm pleased you like it," the Captain said.

"Oh, enjoy it. I certainly do," Mrs. Minford said with a decided nod. "And what of the others at the table? Surely you can all agree that this might be perhaps the most delicious wassail we have ever had the pleasure of enjoying?"

There were nods up and down the table, and murmurs of agreement.

"I am pleased to hear it," the Captain said. "My hope was that I could provide my guests with every enjoyment while you were all here for dinner."

"You are very kind, Captain," Mrs. Minford said. "And how perfect your timing is for a night of merriment."

My heart skipped a beat, and I looked up the table at the Captain.

He seemed perplexed, his brows drawing together. "I am not certain what you mean," he said.

Mrs. Minford sighed rather dramatically. "Oh, Captain…surely you have heard about the tragedy that has befallen our small town?"

A hush fell over the table, a silence that pressed in uncomfortably close.

My gaze, drawn to Lily, recalled our conversation earlier.

How predictable Mrs. Minford is, speaking up about Mr. Morton already.

It was not surprising that she would want to draw attention to herself by bringing up the town's most talked about gossip. It was, of course, a topic on everyone's mind, but Mrs. Minford was, as always, eager to be the first to speak of it.

Lily, tight lipped and stiff chinned, seemed to be of the same mind as me. She regarded Mrs. Minford with a veiled disdain that made my skin begin to itch. Her gaze urged Mrs. Minford's silence, though I knew as well as she that Mrs. Minford was as blind as could be in regards to subtle social cues presented by those around her.

Captain Seymour, surely feeling the gaze of nearly every eye in the room, set his uneasy smile upon his guests, most notably Mrs. Minford. "I have heard of such a thing. Though is a cheerful engagement such as this the sort of place to be speaking of such ill matters?"

My eyes narrowed slightly for a brief moment. *No, that gives nothing away. He might have said the very same if he was guilty, to be sure, but it is a perfectly innocent statement, one that anyone might make in the situation. For who would wish to ruin such a pleasant atmosphere?*

"I agree heartily," said Mr. Clark, beside Lily. He was a distinguished looking man, with dark brows the same shade of black as his thick hair. He glowered across the table at Mrs. Minford; it was no secret that the level-headed Clark family cared little for dramatic tendencies. "We need not spoil such a fine evening with talk of death and deceit."

Mrs. Minford's eyes widened, her gaze sharpening as she met Mr. Clark's.

Tension rose, and the silence grew more deafening.

"But why shouldn't we?" she asked, almost breathless. "Mr. Morton...poor Mr. Morton. Whoever attacked him needs to be brought to justice."

"I agree with you," Mr. Clark said. "But I am confident the police are capable of managing the matter."

Mrs. Minford's eyes narrowed. "Constable Brown is no closer to resolving anything than we are," she said, a sharp note in her words.

"How do you know?" Lily asked, her own brow furrowing. "Have you spoken with him?"

"I have not personally, no," Mrs. Minford said.

A general air of disagreement rose from around the table. Mrs. Clark rolled her eyes toward the ceiling, and Mr. Sawyer shook his head at the far end of the table.

"But the matter is clear, is it not? There has been nothing in the newspaper, and we would have certainly heard if the killer had been caught," Mrs. Minford said.

"That is supposing there *was* a killer in the first place," Mrs. Clark muttered.

"If anyone had heard of the killer's unveiling, it would certainly be Mrs. Minford," said Mr. Newman from his place beside his wife at the same moment Mrs. Clark spoke.

"These matters take time, do they not?" It was Captain Seymour this time, his tone as gentle as possible.

All along the table, eyes drifted back toward him.

I had expected to hear whispers of these matters tonight...but not a discussion quite so outright. Nor so soon.

"During my time in the army, we ran into a few cases like this in the town where we resided. Once it was one of our soldiers, who was killed by a local in protest of our presence. Soon after, it was a young man, also a local, who had been killed in a fight with some raiders who had infiltrated the town in secret. It took the authorities nearly three months to discern the killers and find their hideout."

"It is clear to me that the Captain has an understanding of these matters," Mr. Clark said. "If these situations take time to understand, then we can do our part by being patient, and grieving alongside Mr. Morton's family and friends as they – "

"But what if the killer strikes again?" Mrs. Minford asked, her hand sweeping in front of her. "What if they manage to somehow evade the constable so well that they are never caught?"

"That's preposterous," Mr. Newman said scathingly, shaking his head from side to side. "Are you implying the Constable is incapable?"

"Not at all, I have the utmost confidence in him," Mrs. Minford said.

"Yet you just spoke as if you did not," Mr. Clark said.

Mrs. Minford opened her mouth to speak again, but halted as if someone had struck her. It was her husband's hand upon her arm, and the embarrassed, somewhat pleading look on his face that caused her to cease in her frantic tirade.

"My dear, if you would tell them what you have heard, as opposed to dancing around the issue?" he asked.

I regarded Mr. Minford, wondering how a man such as he had married the woman he had. I thought, as I had many times before, that she must have been a very different woman in her youth. Perhaps she was astonishingly handsome. Perhaps she was wise and careful with her words. Whatever the case, I hoped beyond all hope that he still had love for the poor woman, for living with her would surely be intolerable otherwise.

Mrs. Minford's expression quickly softened and even became somewhat contrite. "Yes, you are right, my dear," she said. She turned back to the rest of the table. "My husband is correct in reminding me that the reason I bring this all up in the first place is because of what I heard only yesterday."

I glanced over at Lily, whose expression was unreadable. Her gaze, as hard as steel, was fixed perfectly on Mrs. Minford.

For not wanting to be involved in this case, my dear sister is certainly paying close attention.

"It seems that Mr. Morton was not stabbed in the street, as was rumored. No…it seems the unfortunate man may have been poisoned."

"Poisoned?" exclaimed Mrs. Newman, her hand clutching her burgundy dress where it lay over her heart.

"Indeed," Mrs. Minford said with a greedy nod as she stared around the table at the shocked expressions. "The poison must have caught up with him as soon as he left the pub."

It was as if I had swallowed ice water. My stomach clenched, and it took all the strength I had not to whip around and stare at Lily in utter dismay.

Mrs. Minford...you can't have –

It astounded me in every way that she would have the audacity – the *gall* – to repeat what she had heard at our shop just the morning before. Information that she had wormed out of us, having eavesdropped on our private conversation.

Even though I could not see her, I felt Lily tense beside me, though not nearly as much as I did, knowing full well that to say anything, to make a gesture of any kind, would be enough to give away that Lily and I knew exactly what she was speaking of.

I waited for Mrs. Minford's gaze to pass over Lily and me, waited for her mouth to open once more.

What will she say?

"Where did you hear such a rumor?" Captain Seymour asked. " A poisoning seems highly unlikely."

"Is it, Captain?" Mrs. Minford asked, her eyes narrowing. "What if I told you that my source heard it from Doctor Webb himself, who examined the body?"

"Good heavens..." Mrs. Clark murmured just a few seats down.

The glee that glittered in Mrs. Minford's eyes was very nearly too much for me to bear.

"But poisoning is such a devious means of killing someone," Mr. Sawyer said from further down the table, picking at his greying beard. It means whoever committed the deed planned it, perhaps for some time – "

"Exactly," Mrs. Minford said. "Exactly my thought as well, Mr. Sawyer."

Lily drummed her fingers on the table, and Captain Seymour cleared his throat.

"It is a tragedy, to be sure," the Captain said. "But perhaps it would be best if we were to move on from such unhappy conversation, and – "

"My apologies for my tardiness – "

A voice at the far side of the room clashed with the Captain's.

I looked up to see the handsome figure of Nash Greenwood standing just inside the doorway to the dining room.

The tension flooded from the room at once, like a puncture in an overfilled wineskin.

"Ah, Mr. Greenwood," Captain Seymour said, stretching out his hand. "How good of you to make it."

Nash Greenwood stepped fully into the room, and I was surprised when my heart skipped slightly. Taller than I remembered, he somehow seemed different now that he wasn't wearing his fire brigadier uniform. He came dressed in a smart suit of deepest green, which made his hair look like honey, gleaming in the light from the lanterns overhead as he walked up to the table.

He smiled easily at those around the table, and from their expressions, it seemed he was already acquainted with almost everyone in attendance.

His eyes fell upon me in his passing, and there they halted. His smile grew ever so slightly bigger, the corners of his eyes wrinkling with warmth and familiarity.

"I am terribly sorry, sir," he said to the Captain, pulling his eyes away from me, though it seemed to be as difficult for him as it was for me. "I was held up at practice when one of my brigadiers managed to injure himself on our way out of the gorge where we were training."

"I'm sorry to hear it. Is he all right?" Captain Seymour asked, getting to his feet and gesturing to a seat just two down from himself, across the table from me.

"Yes, indeed," Nash said. "His pride is wounded far worse than anything else, I assure you."

"Very good," Captain Seymour said with a large smile, though from the tightness of his jaw, it was clear that he still battled his frustrations from the conversation with Mrs. Minford. "Please, come sit down. You are just in time; the meal is about to be served."

He ensured that it was.

The servants returned not even five minutes later with covered silver trays, bringing heady, spicy aromas into the room with them. Each tray was placed in the middle of the table before the cover was removed. None of the contents were what was expected.

"It is quite uncustomary to enjoy pork or beef in India, you see," Captain Seymour explained.

"Didn't you miss it, though?" Mrs. Newman asked.

"To be parted from what you are used to…" I saw that she eyed the dishes before her with clear apprehension, her eyes wide and her lips pursed tightly together.

"Their religion finds it reprehensible," Captain Seymour said. "As I, myself, was an outsider, I could be forgiven my own habits, but I found myself rather fascinated by their food."

"I believe I have sampled this dish before," said Nash, pointing with the end of his fork to a platter before him filled with rice and lamb. "My cousin was stationed for a time in India, as well, you see. He prepared this for us one evening when he was home on leave."

"Ah, yes," the Captain said, beaming at the young man for not rejecting the meal outright. "I'm pleased that this cuisine is not entirely foreign to all here."

I smiled as Nash met my gaze across the table with a small grin. "Not at all, sir. I think you will find that even if these foods are a bit outside the experience of most of your guests, they will enjoy them all the same. Miss Dickinson, you shall certainly try the Captain's offerings, will you not?"

I felt Lily's gaze on my face, as Nash was staring directly at me. "Why yes," I said. "I will be most delighted to try what the Captain has served us."

The meal was excellent, though I found it rather difficult to fully enjoy with the glances my sister insisted on throwing my direction. Disapproval was all

I could make out, and I wondered what, exactly, she was disapproving of.

Of course Mrs. Minford's behavior, as I still cannot believe she mentioned what she had heard from us about Mr. Morton's demise...but what of Nash Greenwood's looks in my direction? Surely she notices them and will question me about them as soon as she is able.

Dinner was no sooner ended when Captain Seymour rose to his feet, insisting on a tour of the rest of his home.

"A means of controlling the direction of conversation, no doubt," Lily said to me under her breath as we rose from the table. "Not that I mind, of course. Mrs. Minford's ability to so ruin my good mood never ceases to astound me."

"Good evening, ladies."

Just as we followed the rest of the group from the room, Nash approached Lily and me.

"Good evening, Mr. Greenwood," Lily said. "I suppose I should not be surprised at your being invited to this party, what with your being the fire chief and all."

"Fire chief?" I asked, looking up at him.

He grinned rather sheepishly. "Indeed. When I met you the other day, I suppose I failed to make mention of it, didn't I?"

"You said you had moved from Sheffield to train the new recruits," I said, smiling at him. "Fire chief is quite the responsibility, however."

"I am honored to have the title," he said with a

small inclination of his head. "So, would you ladies mind terribly if I joined you for the house tour?"

The look that Lily gave me was amused, yet also intrigued. "We would be delighted. Wouldn't we, Iris?"

"Of course, sir. Yes, you must," I said.

The Captain was a little further up ahead of us, already in the middle of a story about a handsome painting of a seaside that he was describing.

He took us through each and every room, and though I could not converse openly with Lily about what we saw, the glances we exchanged were enough for each to acknowledge what the other was seeing. My mind was full, juggling not only the memory of Mrs. Minford's open betrayal of trust, but the possibility that it could still be Captain Seymour who had killed Mr. Morton. Were we, in fact, in the house of a murderer? Was the Captain so startled by Mrs. Minford's words because he felt as if he had been discovered in his own home, at his own dining table? Or was he simply as shaken as everyone else had been by the subject?

If I was honest with myself, I could not put the full blame on Mrs. Minford. She was the one who had put the wretched idea in our heads in the first place that it might have been the Captain, but how could we be sure we could trust her suspicions? Her rumors had been wrong many times before in the past. Why should we listen to her now?

We strode from room to room; the drawing room, the parlor, the larder, the library. The Captain then took us upstairs to the second floor, which was just as lavish as the first.

"And here we have the guest room, which I must admit is my favorite room in the entire house," the Captain said to our group, gesturing through a door at the south end of the hall. "And across the hall is the study, which is my personal place of enjoyment. Inside you will find perhaps the largest collection of bidri-ware vases in all of England."

Mrs. Minford peered into the guest room, her husband close behind her.

Lily took hold of my elbow and drew me toward the study. "I should like to keep my distance from Mrs. Minford, lest I utterly lose sense of myself and confront her here and now."

She spoke in a low voice, just loud enough so I might hear her.

The study was a warm space, with lanterns dotted about; on the shelves, on the desk, on the windowsill on the opposite wall. As exotic as they were, they brought coziness to the space with their colored glass, the candles within flickering happily.

"What a comfortable space," Nash said, following us into the room. "And my heavens, I should think that the Captain has a library to rival any in town."

"Perhaps," Lily said. "I should wonder what sort of books he likes to read. A man's collection of books describes his character a great deal."

"Indeed it does," I said, peering at the spines of

some of the texts before me. I slid the first tome that caught my eye from the shelf. "Dickens, of course."

"And here we have Hardy, Thackeray, and George Eliot," Nash said, using the tip of his finger to peruse through the novels. "Rather predictable, if you ask me."

Lily drew nearer to me, glancing briefly over at Nash. "I should be honest, sister," she whispered, pretending to pull another book from the shelf to examine. "I have not laid eyes upon anything that might suggest the Captain suspicious."

"Neither have I," I said. "Not a thing that might give him away as a killer. What of Bronte, Mr. Greenwood?" I asked, a little louder. "Still considered predictable?"

"I believe so, yes," he said, scratching his chin. "Though I imagine he would have sought after perfectly ordinary literature during his stay in India, if only for a bit of comfort from home. Wouldn't you agree?"

"Oh, certainly," I said. "That is a perfectly reasonable conclusion"

I admired our male companion's profile, and the concentration that furrowed his brow as he stared at the shelf before him. His jaw, still as strong as ever, and his steely eyes…so piercing and intense –

"He is quite handsome," Lily murmured, a smirk playing in the corner of her mouth.

My face flushed scarlet.

"You know," Nash said, striding over toward us as

Mr. and Mrs. Newman entered the room. "Captain Seymour is a very interesting fellow, is he not? I wouldn't say peculiar, but certainly interesting...he must have especially enjoyed his time in India to turn his home into a museum spectacle for all his collections."

"I thought the very same," I said. "Those black vases inlaid with silver must be the bidriware he spoke of. It's lovely, to be sure. However, I am not certain I would have wanted to bother with the trouble of bringing so much of it back home..." I noted at least a dozen vases that looked the same, only different in size.

"Not only that, but it seems every inch of his home is covered in such things," Lily said. "To each his own, I suppose."

Nash glanced back over his shoulder at Mr. and Mrs. Newman, who were busy examining the largest of the vases that sat upon his desk. "What say you to this rumor of Captain Seymour being the one to poison poor Mr. Morton?"

I very nearly swallowed my tongue. "How did you – you weren't even here for that discussion – "

"I overheard Mr. and Mrs. Clark speaking of it as we observed the parlor," he said. "It all seems rather ridiculous, if you ask me, including the notion that the poor man was poisoned in the first place."

"Mrs. Minford claims that the Doctor who examined the body is the one who proclaimed he was poisoned," Lily said.

I stared at her, my heart quickening. *Does she mean to draw attention to us?*

"Truly?" Nash asked. "And is her word to be trusted? Because it seems to me that she is the sort of silly woman who makes these things up half the time, and is right even less of the time."

"You have the measure of her character," Lily said.

"She is as easy to read as one of these books," Nash said, prodding the spine of *Our Mutual Friend*. "I would sooner believe the claims of a serpent."

I opened my mouth.

It would be so easy for me to open up to him, to share with him our findings and thoughts on the matter. If he has already heard almost as much as we have, then what can the harm be?

One look at Lily's face, however, told me how unwise that would be.

"Miss Iris?" Nash asked, blinking at me. "Is everything all right? You seem to be quite pale all of a sudden."

No...it would be unwise. Lily wishes to remain discreet. And sharing our thoughts with him would be as far from that as possible.

"I'm fine," I said with a forced smile, inclining my head. "Thank you for your concern."

Lily's expression was one of question. She knew precisely the struggle that passed through my mind.

She wonders why I would trust him so readily, when we hardly know him.

I swallowed hard as the three of us headed back toward the door.

Why was I so willing to trust him? Why did he give me that feeling?

"Oh, pardon me, Miss Dickinson," he said as we both made to step through the door at the same time. He smiled, and stepped aside for me to pass.

It's that smile. His smile promises that he would never betray anyone.

And yet, looks could be deceiving…it was best for me to guard myself against him.

…For now.

11

Lily and I returned home that evening at half past eleven. Tired and overwhelmed from the dinner party, we agreed to discuss what we had learned – regardless of how little it was – after we had a full night's sleep. I had no desire to argue; the heavy food had left me content and exhausted.

The next morning was Sunday, and we woke as we always did by six, in preparations for church that morning. We took our tea together as we ate some bread and jam, dressed and left the house just before eight.

Rain was imminent; the dark, roiling clouds up overhead made that clear. We grabbed both our umbrellas before we headed out into the chilly, morning air.

"Autumn will soon be giving way to winter, mark my words," Lily said, sliding her arm through my own, pulling me close for warmth. "Oh, how I despise the cold."

"So you say every year, dear sister, and yet you cherish your time by the fire with a good book, a cup of tea in hand," I said, nudging her affectionately.

She smiled at me from beneath her bonnet.

We made our way up the street, seeing many other townsfolk leaving their homes at the same time, also on their way to the church up on the hill.

"Well, now, sister, what say you about last night?" Lily asked as we walked along, our breaths forming small puffs of clouds which trailed behind us. "Do you believe our dear Captain Seymour capable of such villainous acts?"

"No," I said, my brow furrowing. "But I will tell you who I am exceedingly disappointed in. Mrs. Minford."

Lily's arm tensed in my own. "I understand. I, too, am frustrated. She has always been a busybody, but I have never known her to be quite so untrustworthy."

"To speak openly about something that we had discussed in private..." I said sadly. "I did not believe her to be capable of such treachery."

"If you will remember, dear sister, she did overhear *our* conversation in the first place," Lily said.

"Eavesdropping," I said, shaking my head. "That surprised me, indeed."

"What ever happened to the sweet woman who took the time to teach you needlepoint?" Lily asked.

I frowned. "I don't know. I would much rather her

be a little too nosy…instead of this much less desirable version of herself."

We walked in silence for a few moments, letting the reality of what had happened the night before settle over us.

"At least she didn't tell them all who it was she had overheard the information from," I said. "It could have been much worse."

Lily remained quiet as we turned onto Church Street, still keeping our distance from any of the other families also on their way to Sunday service.

"I suppose we should not be surprised," she said, tucking a lock of her dark hair behind her ear; the chilled wind had pulled it loose. "Mrs. Minford always has to have her gossip, and this might be the biggest story she has ever heard of in Grangehurst. It is likely keeping her up at night."

Despite the derision in her words, the truth of what she said softened my heart somewhat.

"Perhaps we should forgive her actions and dismiss them as nothing more than one aspect of her character." I said. "We must continue to do business with her, after all, mustn't we?"

Lily's brow furrowed. "…I suppose we must," she said, glaring at the cobbles beneath her feet. "Iris, you are irritatingly forgiving sometimes. Do her actions not infuriate you as they do me?"

"They certainly do," I said. "But what am I to do about them now?"

"We must pray that she never reveals who she heard these things from," Lily said. "Lest we find ourselves drawing the very attention we have been trying to avoid –"

"Good morning, Miss Lily, Miss Iris," came a voice behind us.

My heart skipped. Had we been overheard? Were our worries of being discovered to be met by our own folly?

I looked behind me and found Mr. and Mrs. Clark, and their three young children, coming up the path toward us.

"Good morning," I said, and Lily did likewise.

Mrs. Clark, carrying her youngest, Thomas, stepped up beside me. "It was quite a party last night, wasn't it?" she asked. "I've never seen such a display in all my life."

"Nor I, to be sure," Lily said. "I was astounded at the Captain's home. He has certainly taken great care in making things just so."

"And all of the furnishings," Mrs. Clark said, her eyes wide, absentmindedly adjusting the wriggling infant in her arms. "It must have cost him a fortune."

"A pittance for him, my dear, as a man of some means," her husband said, leaning around his wife to nod to both Lily and I. "I imagine it was one of the last great pleasures of his time there to select so much to bring home with him."

"It must have taken an entire ship," Lily said.

"I believe it must have," Mr. Clark said with a toothy grin.

"And what of you and the good Mr. Greenwood?" Mrs. Clark asked, eyes darting back and forth between Lily and I as she changed the topic of conversation. "I had never been introduced to the man until last night."

"Oh," I said, looking down at the buttons on my dress. "Yes, I – I met him just a few days prior."

"He had come into the shop, and I made him a new shirt," Lily said. "His was rather tired and worn. As chief fire brigadier, he certainly needed something more fitting."

"He's quite charming," Mr. Clark said. "Very agreeable sort of fellow. Just the kind that Grangehurst needed."

I felt Mrs. Clark's gaze on the side of my face. "He seemed friendly with you, Miss Iris. One might think he was rather fond of you."

My face flushed, but Lily spoke before I could.

"He seems the flirtatious type, to be sure," Lily said with a firm nod. "The sort that my sister has far too much sense to entertain."

"Oh, he didn't strike me as such," Mr. Clark said, lips pursed, shaking his head. "I thought him rather level. Honorable man."

"As did I," Mrs. Clark said. "I thought to myself that you might certainly make a worse match for yourself, either of you."

Lily's face screwed up in distaste. "He must be nearly ten years younger than I," she said. "No, if he were to take interest in either of us, it would surely be my sister. She is the prettier."

"Do not be so hard on yourself," I said, furrowing my brow as I looked at my sister. "Lily, you have so many good qualities –"

"You know how I feel about flattery, sister," Lily interrupted with a stern look. "In any case, I am well beyond the age for such nonsense."

"Oh, come now, Miss Lily," Mrs. Clark said. "You do not wish to marry?"

"Certainly not," Lily said. "When a woman has made a comfortable life for herself, there is no reason she should feel it necessary…"

Her words trailed off as we rounded the corner of Church Street and Elderberry Lane, where a crowd of people appeared just before the gate leading up to the churchyard.

"Good heavens, what is happening?" Mrs. Clark asked.

It took only a moment to realize that they were all gathered out in front of Constable Brown's home.

A cold chill trickled down my spine. *This couldn't have anything to do with the gossip at last night's dinner party, could it?*

"But how are we to sleep at night?" called Mrs. Newman, clutching the hand of her youngest daughter. "How can we feel safe, knowing there is a dangerous killer roaming our streets?"

Lily and I stopped walking, hanging back to observe the group of nearly two dozen townsfolk.

"What is taking so long?" asked a young man who I thought might be the middle son of Mr. Sawyer. "Why hasn't the attacker been caught yet?"

"Everyone, calm down!"

The Constable's voice carried out over the crowd, and he soon appeared on the front steps of his home. He was dressed, as the rest of the crowd was, in his best Sunday clothes, a suit of charcoal grey.

The murmurs of the crowd quieted, all eyes on him as he surveyed them.

"Everyone, please remain calm. Everything necessary is being done to get to the bottom of this matter – "

"There are children in this town, Constable. Or have you forgotten?" Mr. Newman asked. "Children whose mothers and fathers are terrified to let them out to play, afraid that they might not come home safely."

"Lily," I whispered, turning my gaze upon my sister. "We must – "

She squeezed my arm, her fingernails digging into my flesh. "We must do *nothing*. Remember what we discussed," she said, just under her breath.

I stared at the group, hearing more fears spouted off from those in the crowd.

"My business has struggled because of this situation," the owner of the pub protested. "I cannot very well serve patrons who are too afraid to step foot inside my establishment, afraid they, too, might end up dead."

"I understand your concerns, truly I do," Constable Brown said, his arms outstretched, pleading with the crowd before him. "I assure you we are doing all we can. Now if you will please excuse us, my family and I would like to continue – "

"Is it true that Mr. Morton was poisoned?" asked Miss Baldwin, who had pushed her way to the front of the crowd.

A stiff gust of wind blew down through the street, stirring up the skirts of the women and the coat tails of the men.

Constable Brown's gaze looked past the crowd, down the street...and fell upon me as I stood there.

And all I could do was listen, horrified.

"If he was poisoned, that means someone living in this town has thought through and committed a murder," said Miss Baldwin. "How can any of us rest when we don't understand how or why this happened?"

"Or what if this was someone passing through?" Mrs. Newman asked, her face paling. "Then we will likely never know who it was!"

"I want to know what is going to be done," Mr. Sawyer's son said, red in the face. "What measures will be taken to bring this matter to a close?"

"There is a great deal about this that we don't understand," the Constable said, raising his voice so that he could be heard over all the others. "You have my word, however, that all efforts are being directed at solving this case. The culprit will be brought to justice."

Constable Brown's gaze shifted back over the crowd to fall upon me once again.

The glint in his gaze, the sharpness of his expression gave me pause.

We stared at one another for a few moments, before the tug of Lily's hand on my arm drew my attention away.

"Come along, sister. We are going to be late," she said gently.

I nodded, looking back up at the Constable.

Surely he could not think that I was the one who allowed this information to get out...could he?

How could he think otherwise? It *was* my fault. I had chosen to speak about it in a very public space, in the middle of the day in our shop while we worked. If I had had any sense, I might have held my tongue and waited until Lily and I were well enough alone, up in our own rooms. We might have discussed it more openly, considered the information...but then have been done with it.

"It's my fault..." I said under my breath as we made our way through the churchyard. The wind blew, and the bells in the steeple began to chime. "It's entirely my fault."

"No, no," Lily murmured as we stepped away from the Clarks. "Don't say that."

"It is, though," I said, coming to a stop.

Grangehurst was always at its most beautiful when viewed from this spot. It sprawled out below us, gently rolling down the hill all the way to the cliff's edge, where the river snaked through the gorge below, the most constant aspect of our small town.

The wind swept across the churchyard, bringing the scent of the falling leaves and the rich, moist earth.

"If I had not said anything within earshot of Mrs. Minford – "

"How could you have known?" Lily asked. "She walked in just as you were speaking."

"But I should have had more sense," I said. "I might have saved everyone so much trouble. Did you see how many people were there, gathering in front of the Constable's house? And the way he looked at me…he *knew* it was I who said something. How could it have been anyone else? No one else would have had the chance to overhear it."

"If Doctor Webb had so little sense as to speak before seeing who was in the room as he entered, then he is as much to blame. If not more so," Lily said.

I frowned. "I'm not certain of that."

"Well, I am," Lily said. "What's more, you do not know if he said anything to anyone else after leaving the room with the Constable. Another person might have spread the rumor just as easily."

I shook my head. I knew, as well as she did, that was not true. Mrs. Minford had surely been the one to spread the news all over town before the day was out yesterday.

"Thank you anyway, sister, for trying to make me feel better about it all," I said.

I turned and started toward the church, my heart

heavy. Shame hung over me like a shroud and I feared what was to come next.

What harm have I done? What might have been prevented had I had more sense?

It did little good to dwell on the questions. It wasn't as if I could change things now.

12

I had spent most of the Sundays of my life sitting in the pew beside my sister, listening to Reverend Michaels speak from the Word in a practical and informative manner. Often, when I struggled with something in my personal life, I felt as if the reverend had written his sermon using my own experiences as his inspiration.

That morning after the Captain's dinner party was no different.

Worrying about my responsibility in the town's discovery of Mr. Morton's poisoning, I sat in silence as Reverend Michaels began to speak of the story of Judas, and his deception.

I glanced around the room. *Was Mr. Morton's killer sitting here this morning? Was there a Judas among us?*

There was, of course. Whether or not they were sitting in the sanctuary with the rest of us was yet to be determined but a dangerous person certainly existed somewhere in our town.

My gaze drifted across the room. Almost every eye was fixed on the reverend standing at the front. Some congregants, like Mr. Sawyer, glanced down at the Bibles in their hands. Others, like Mrs. Newman, were leaning in close and murmuring to her children, encouraging them to stay quiet.

I noticed Captain Seymour, sitting on the opposite side of the room. It seemed he had made a friend of Nash Greenwood, who sat beside him.

My heart stirred, and I had trouble distinguishing whether it was a good or a bad sign. Was I pleased to see Nash, as I had been the night before? Or was I worried, seeing him sitting with the Captain as he was?

There was absolutely nothing last night indicating the Captain might be a murderer. I wasn't expecting to find a bottle lying out, labeled "poison", but I thought perhaps he might have given something away to indicate guilt.

Lily and I had seen nothing apart from an unusual man and the rare trinkets he had brought home.

Perhaps we should have crept away from the others... looked inside cupboards, or even in that elaborate trunk in his sitting room...

It made little difference now.

The Captain's face, seeming free from any guilt, faced toward the Reverend.

If he was the one to commit the crime, how could he look up at the minister the way he is? How could he seem so untroubled?

A cough echoed throughout the room, followed closely by a rather profound sniffle.

I was not the only one to glance in the direction of the sound.

"Henrietta Morton," Lily whispered to me.

I looked over at her, and saw her eyes focused on a row closer to the front than ours, her gaze fixed on the back of the head of the woman who had let out such a terrible cough.

It was indeed Henrietta, Mr. Morton's wife.

Curious that she would be here. I thought she was visiting family out of town?

"I imagine she received news of what transpired in her absence," Lily murmured to me, clearly reading my thoughts on my face.

"That's a speedy return, is it not?" I asked in a whisper. "In such a few short days...it's almost as if she knew it was to happen, and did not want to appear indifferent."

Lily's eyes widened, and she gave me a small, silent nod.

I exhaled slowly through my nose, returning my gaze to Reverend Michaels. I had very nearly forgotten about Henrietta Morton.

The wife who had deserted Mr. Morton...

I could not see her very well from where I sat, but as she turned her head slightly to the side I noticed her dab at her eyes with her handkerchief, moved to tears, it seemed, by Reverend Michaels' message.

My heart sank as I continued to watch her.

How are we to discern who the real culprit is? How can we know for certain?

Perhaps it was not our responsibility to know. Perhaps all we had to do was wait patiently for Constable Brown to discover the truth.

The service ended, and it was not long after Reverend Michaels dismissed the congregation that I heard murmurs of luncheon and tea.

"Wonderful message, that," Mr. Clark said as he and Mrs. Clark walked past our pew. "Just the sort of thing I needed to hear."

"Well, shall we stop at the grocer's?" Lily asked. "I am in need of some yeast. I thought fresh bread with our soup tonight might be good."

"That would be nice, yes," I said.

We moved away from the pew together, falling in behind Mrs. Hobbs, who glanced over her shoulder more than once.

"My apologies, ladies," she said kindly, though it was quite clear her attention was fully on something behind us.

We stepped out into the late morning air. The wind had died down, but the cold still lingered.

"I am certain we shall freeze before winter ever arrives here," Lily said, pulling her gloves over her thin, boney fingers. "We need not even see the first of November."

I unwrapped the scarf in my hands looking for my own gloves. "Oh, heavens," I said. "I believe I left my gloves in our pew." I looked back through the open door of the church. "I should fetch them. I won't be but a moment."

"Very well, I shall wait here," Lily said.

The sanctuary had emptied quickly, everyone eagerly anticipating a warm meal to soothe their chilled bones. My footsteps echoed across the space, and the dust kicked up by everyone's footsteps danced in the beams of light from the stained glass windows.

I walked up through the pew where Lily and I had been sitting, seeing my grey gloves resting there.

Just as I stooped to grab them, the sound of a woman bursting into tears filled the room.

I froze where I stood, my heartbeat quickening.

"There, now," came Reverend Michaels' voice. "It's quite all right to be distressed. It is perfectly natural, given what has occurred."

My face flooding with color, I turned to hurry from the pew. This was surely a private matter that someone would be perturbed if I overheard.

"I am beside myself, Reverend," the woman said, sniffling once more. "How am I to bear this? How am I to face it?"

With a skip of my heartbeat, I stopped just inside the row of pews.

It's Mrs. Morton!

"He was your husband," Reverend Michaels said. "Even if you were living separately at the time that he passed away, it does not surprise me at all that you still cared for him in your heart."

"I did," Henrietta Morton said, her voice cracking.

She sobbed a few times. "I do. I still loved him. I should have told him. I should have – "

Her cries echoed across the vaulted ceilings, which made them sound even more sorrowful than they were.

My throat grew tight, and guilt washed over me. *I am intruding on this moment...*

Even still, I could not bring myself to stop, as a thought far in the back of my mind held me firmly in place.

What if she is the one who killed him? What if this is her confession?

"I treated him so poorly..." she said after a moment, gathering herself long enough to draw in a few, shaky breaths. "I despised him, Reverend. I hated the ground he walked upon. He *ruined* me. Ruined my life, the lives of our children. His poor decisions, his indiscretion, his selfish refusal to seek the help he needed. He would not think of his family...he would not think of *me*. And now look where it got him?"

I glanced around, certain that someone would walk in and catch me listening to this conversation. My feet, however, refused to move.

Could she be the one?

"It's all right, Mrs. Morton," Reverend Michaels said, though I noticed a hint of worry rising in his voice. "You cannot blame yourself – "

"But I do, sir..." she said, half hysterical. "I *do* blame myself! How could I not? For it *is my fault!*"

I gripped the back of the pew beside me for support.

She did kill him!

"I am responsible for his death!" she cried.

My mouth dried up. My eyes refused to blink. I could only stare at the wall across from me, the candles burning low in their sconces beside the windows, their dying, flickering light the only movement in the whole room.

She burst into tears once again.

"Mrs. Morton..." Reverend Michaels said. The uncertainty was clear in his voice.

"I am responsible!" she wailed again.

"No," Reverend Michaels said. "You are not responsible. Unless you are telling me that you were the one to creep up on him in the darkness and take his life?"

The crying eased for a moment. "I...I wasn't here, I was out of town, with my cousin – "

The conviction in her voice could not be mistaken.

But surely someone capable of murder would be capable of lying about it?

"Then you must calm these feelings, and forgive yourself," Reverend Michaels said. "Had I known that my message would have been so troubling for you today, I might have chosen a different one...though I should not discount the Lord's hand in these matters."

"Iris?"

I very nearly jumped out of my skin at the voice behind me.

Whirling around, I found Lily standing there, her eyebrows knit together.

My face flooded with color.

"What are you doing in here?" she asked. "I thought something might have happened, you were taking so long."

I hurried to her, laying my hand on her arm. The action silenced her.

Dropping my voice to a whisper, I said, "Come, I shall tell you what I heard when we are safely back home."

13

"So..." Lily said, pacing back and forth across the sitting room after we arrived home a short time later. "You do not think it was Mr. Morton's wife who killed him."

The wind had picked up once again, rattling against the windows with such force that I had begun to worry that the shutters would be ripped from the exterior of the building. The sun had not even been seen throughout the whole of the day, and it was almost as if it had forgotten how to shine in the first place.

I picked up my needlepoint that I had set aside the night before. I had wanted to practice stitching a lily before attempting one on Mrs. Newman's hat. "No, she struck me as an innocent woman whose grief was genuine."

Lily's silence greeted me, and for a moment, I wasn't quite sure what to think.

When I looked up at her, I saw the worry between her brows, the wrinkles in her forehead as she turned at the door to the kitchen, retracing her steps back in front of the fireplace, all the way down to the door to the bedroom.

"And she could not have been pretending in order to cast suspicion away from herself?" Lily asked.

I sighed, setting the needlepoint down on the couch beside me. "You have asked me this same question three times now," I pointed out. "She said herself that she wasn't the one to kill him."

"Yes, of course. Murderers are nothing if not honest." My sister's sniff sounded decidedly sarcastic. "Anyway, you told me that she feels responsible for his death."

"She feels her choices are what drove him to his death," I said. "Her deepest regret was abandoning him when he needed her most." I shook my head. "You should have heard the agony in her voice…"

Lily did not look particularly moved. "I suppose we shall know for sure when Constable Brown finally has a chance to speak with her, if he hasn't already…" she said, folding her arms, staring fixedly at a point on the back wall. "Until then, it seems we are back to the Captain."

"How can we accuse him any further?" I asked. "Without any more proof, I mean. All we have is Mrs. Minford's word to go on, and that is about as stable as a boat made of sugar."

Lily stopped, and a brightness came into her eyes.

"Iris, you said that it was Doctor Webb who examined the body, yes?" she asked.

"Yes," I said. "Why?"

"The answer is quite simple, then," she said, a renewed determination in her steps. She turned and marched into the kitchen, and a moment later, I heard the kettle being set onto the stove. She had come to some sort of resolution. "We must go and see the doctor ourselves."

"I thought you wanted to remain at a discreet distance?" I asked, getting to my feet and following her into the kitchen.

"We are," Lily said, glancing over her shoulder as she pulled the tea from its home in the cupboard. "We are simply going as concerned citizens. Let us allow Mrs. Minford's egregious actions to work in our favor."

I WAS STILL CONFUSED at my sister's change of heart as we sat patiently inside Doctor Webb's clinic early the next morning. The secretary at the front asked no questions when Lily asked if we could see Doctor Webb, only telling us that he wouldn't be able to give us a great deal of time.

"We do not need very long," I said. "Only to ask him a few questions about something very important."

My mind raced as a nurse appeared from a door off the small waiting room, calling us back to see the doctor. *Surely he will not believe us to be merely concerned citizens. What sort of person would come directly to the doctor to ask about how someone in town has died?*

Doctor Webb's office sat at the back of the building with a western facing window, which might have been pleasant, absorbing some of the late afternoon sun. There was no sun to be seen, however, as the storm that had begun the day before had kindled itself into a menacing affair.

Just as we had taken our seats in the wooden chairs along the back wall, the door swung inward, and in Doctor Webb came.

"Ah, I'm surprised to see you here, Miss Dickinson," Doctor Webb said to my sister, walking up to her and giving her a full glance up and down, his icy blue eyes squinting behind his thick glasses. "And you, Miss Iris. What can I do for you? Have you caught a case of the sniffles? Or perhaps the chills have set in? Wouldn't surprise me, given this wretched weather we are having."

"No, sir, but thank you for your concern," Lily said. "My sister and I have some questions for you." She glanced at me, her gaze sharp.

Are you certain you wish to do this? How can we deny our own involvement in the matter now?

"We want to know about the poison that was found in Mr. Morton's body," Lily said.

Doctor Webb's eyes narrowed, and his relative indifference disappeared. At once, his gaze shifted to me. "I have heard that everyone in town knows about this. I'm surprised at you, Miss Iris. Going about spreading rumors – "

I opened my mouth to protest, but Lily was quicker than I.

"My sister did no such thing. You have Mrs. Minford to thank for that, as she managed to overhear Iris telling me what you had said."

My face flooded with color. It seemed we were no longer here under the guise of *concerned citizens*. "I am sorry, Doctor Webb, but the whole matter had me quite shaken, and I had to confide in my sister. Surely you can understand that?"

Doctor Webb's wrinkles deepened, a dark look passing over his face.

"I suppose I have no one to blame but myself," he said. "How can I be angry with you for being overheard when that is precisely what I managed to do as well?"

Some of the tension around my heart eased, and I breathed a small sigh of relief.

"Why do you ladies trouble yourself about the poison?" he asked, his gaze shifting back to Lily. "These are matters that really should be left to the proper authorities."

An expression I could not identify crossed my sister's usually stern face. It took me a moment to realize she was attempting to look fearful, a pretense that did not come naturally to her.

"I am concerned for our safety," Lily said. "The murder happened so close to our shop that I worry we might be targeted next. I, for one, would very much like to know how to prepare myself and my sister against something so insidious."

Doctor Webb chewed the inside of his lip. "Is that so?" he asked.

"Please, sir," I said. "This matter has the entire town in an uproar. Friends are suspecting friends, and it seems that no one feels safe, even in their own homes any longer. As two women living alone, we…we simply wish to know as much as possible in order to set our minds at ease."

Doctor Webb hesitated. I could see his good sense as a physician warring with something else inside him, perhaps his natural chivalry, or even simply a desire to gossip. "If I were to tell you what I know, you must promise to keep the knowledge to yourselves," he said. "The investigation is not yet finished, and my involvement with it is technically over now. I will tell you right now, as well, that I do not know who the killer was, only that it was indeed poison that killed the unfortunate victim."

Lily said, "Whatever you feel able to share, we promise to keep the matter within these walls."

"Indeed," I said. "We shan't tell a soul."

And this is a vow I mean to keep. Mrs. Minford shall not catch wind of this.

Doctor Webb drew in a deep breath through his nose before reaching for another chair and pulling it around in front of us, firmly planting himself upon it.

"The poison is something I've taken to calling 'The

Kiss of Death', as it apparently entered the body easily, but spread quite quickly," Doctor Webb said.

"If the poison acted so swiftly, how was he able to stumble out into the street after taking it in?" I asked. "He seemed perfectly alive as he wandered about, singing."

"I imagine whoever gave it to him made quite sure that he was very drunk indeed," Doctor Webb said. "And then distracted him so that he was unaware of their actions."

Lily's brow furrowed. "That seems rather strange, doesn't it? How did this go unmissed by anyone else at the pub?"

"We don't know that there were no witnesses in the pub, do we?" Doctor Webb asked rather tersely. "As I said, I know nothing more than what I have shared with the Constable. And he has not taken the liberty of sharing anything else with me."

"You speak as if this poison was something strange," I said. "What about it sets it apart from others?"

"I did not find traces of the sorts of poisons I am familiar with," Doctor Webb said. "I searched for medicines that are widely available and lethal in high doses, as I am well aware of the sorts of household items a killer might resort to. However, this poison contained properties unlike any I have encountered in all my years – "

The door to Doctor Webb's office opened suddenly, and a young man with dark hair and glasses stepped inside. He had a narrow face, and his body was as thin as a rail.

"Oh, Doctor Webb, my apologies," the young man said, his dark eyes widening in worry. "I did not realize you had patients."

"It's quite all right, William," Doctor Webb said. "William is my assistant, training to be a doctor himself one day. Aren't you, William?"

"Yes, sir," William said, bowing his head timidly, his shoulders hunching.

"Bright, he is. Well versed in natural medicine. And he's got a good eye, too. If it weren't for him, we never would have spotted the injection site."

William looked embarrassed at the praise. "It was nothing, sir. I am sure you yourself would eventually have noticed the small syringe mark."

Syringe mark? This is a new piece of information. Perhaps it is lucky that we are here at this moment.

"Well, perhaps I might have spotted the mark in the end, but the thought of Mr. Morton being killed by poison had not even occurred to me yet. I was still searching for signs of blunt force trauma," Doctor Webb said.

"Well done then, young man," Lily said. "You may be the very reason that the culprit is found."

William nodded in awkward acknowledgement, still seeming shy of the attention. "Doctor Webb, I need to get back to my research, but when you have a moment – "

"Yes, yes, I'll come see your progress," Doctor Webb said.

"Thank you," William said. "If you all will excuse me..."

He bowed to us, and hurried from the room without another word.

Doctor Webb returned to the subject at hand. "The authorities will sort this matter out, don't you ladies distress yourselves about that. The poison is the key, though I must admit anyone could have administered the needle..."

"Perhaps," Lily said. "But I imagine there would not be many in this town who would have access to such a bizarre poison, yes?"

"No, I imagine not," Doctor Webb said. "I shall be very interested in finding out exactly who was responsible for this dark deed."

Lily and I exchanged glances. The doctor was not the only one who would like an answer to that question.

14

"There is only one way to find out if Captain Seymour is responsible," I said over dinner that night.

Lily looked up from her bowl of stew that I had made, her spoon hovering just above the steaming, meaty meal. A slice of carrot slid off and back into the broth. "Oh?" she asked. "And what might that be?"

I set my own spoon down, and folded my hands on the table before me. "We must go to the library, and see what we can find out about this poison."

Lily's eyes narrowed, but her distant gaze told me she considered my suggestion. "And why do you assume that we will find anything at our small library?" she asked. "It is likely quite limited in its available information."

"I realize it may be," I said. "But at the very least, it is a place to start, is it not?"

Lily sighed, looking down. "Iris, I am beginning to

regret my decision to get involved in this matter. From speaking with Doctor Webb, it seems that the proper authorities are doing all they can."

I nodded. "I imagine they are. But you were the one who said that in order to ensure our own reputations were not sullied, we needed to help them find the killer."

"Yes, but even Doctor Webb is uncertain about the poison's origin," Lily said. "How are we then to discern it?"

"The very least we can do is to try," I said.

After a little more coaxing, Lily finally agreed to accompany me to the library. A small building down near the edge of the river, it held more books than many of the other libraries in surrounding villages. The outer walls, the bricks aged from the spray of the river, were covered in ivy that snaked up the bricks, following them almost as if they had been guided there by hand.

"It has been years since I have set foot inside this building," I said. The librarian's desk still sat at the far side of the room, in front of the row of windows. The door to the non-fiction books stood open off to the right, as it always was. The novels and poetry section resided in the old tower in the eastern side of the building, and the local periodicals were lined in a neat row on a shelf beside the door. "Perhaps not since I was a young woman."

"You are still a young woman," Lily said with reproof.

"Not nearly as young," I said. "Being very nearly thirty, dear sister."

Lily gave me an apologetic look as we stepped inside.

We didn't spend a great deal of time speaking with Mrs. Lowell, the librarian, though she would have been glad to talk for a long while. Excited to see some of the town's "young people" as she called us, she was all too eager to help us.

"India, dears?" Mrs. Lowell asked. "What sort of information do you want to know about India?"

Lily and I glanced at one another. There was a warning in Lily's gaze.

"Do you remember Captain Seymour?" I asked. "It seems he spent his twenty year tour in the military in India. We had a lovely dinner party with him a few nights ago, and we have been quite curious about some of the things he spoke of."

I could see the approval in Lily's face, a smile tugging at the corner of her mouth.

"I heard he was back in town…" Mrs. Lowell said, glowering. "Never much approved of the man myself. Neither did my husband. He thought Seymour was a bit too oily for civilized company."

"I certainly find him to be a fairly strange fellow," Lily said. "I should like to learn more about India so as to understand just what it was about it that he misses so much."

"Very well," Mrs. Lowell said. "Well, allow me to show you where you might find some information."

She led us back to the door to the non-fiction section, where ancient shelves stood in tight, dark rows. There was one lone window in the room, which cast very little light throughout the narrow aisles, and the scent of dust and ink hung in the air.

"I love the smell of old books," Lily said in a hushed voice, as if speaking at a normal volume would disturb the books.

I would have agreed, but Mrs. Lowell had brought us to the section we were looking for. She left us a few moments later to look.

"Well...here we are," Lily said.

We exchanged apprehensive glances. Where were we to begin looking?

We decided to start at the most logical place; the beginning.

Pulling books from the shelf, we brought them to the small table near the door, tipped them onto the surface, and began to read.

At first, we weren't sure where to look. We examined chapters about Indian culture, including rituals and holidays. We examined popular foods and spices, as well as medical practices and procedures. It wasn't long before we found information about Indian laws and customs, which quickly lead to crimes and punishments.

"Here we are," Lily said, her finger stopping halfway down a page. "It says here that a man once was arrested for murdering nineteen different people over the span of thirty years, and it was assumed that the cause of these deaths were poisonings, given their difficulty to trace."

"That's good," I said, leaning forward, pushing aside my own book about herbal treatments for wounds. "What was the poison used?"

Lily's eyes scanned the page, and then she sighed heavily. "Cyanide," she said. "Quite obviously. And I'm certain Doctor Webb would recognize cyanide."

"Almost anyone would, I imagine," I said, my lip curling in distaste. "And that sort of poisoning wouldn't take very long to take effect, would it?" The thought of a body decomposing right before our eyes made me quite grateful that it was not what we had stumbled upon.

We continued to search.

"We aren't getting anywhere..." I said a few hours later, shoving the book away.

The sun, having finally made an appearance after days of hiding, had begun to set. The room, bathed in its late afternoon light, sweltered. Sweat clung to my brow, and I was very nearly mad with the effort of wiping it away. My handkerchief was sodden.

"Now, now, there's no need for a tantrum..." Lily said, squinting down at the miniscule writing on the page she poured over.

"I am *not* having a tantrum," I said. "But we are not finding anything. Not anything at all."

"I thought we might not," Lily said, sitting back in her chair, eyeing the page with distaste. "We would have been better off traveling to London or Oxford and going through the larger libraries there."

I glared at her. *I wish her talent for tact outweighed her desire to always inform me when she is right and I am not.*

I sighed, pushing my anger aside, knowing it to be rooted in the heat and the long hours sitting in the same, rigid chair. "Well, then...what are we to do?"

"I think it might be time to trust this case to the police," Lily said, closing the book with a decided *snap*. "Wash our hands of the matter entirely, and move on with our lives."

"You aren't frightened?" I asked. "The killer could very well still be in town, and if they took the time to formulate a murder, then they..." I trailed off.

"What?" Lily asked, her brow furrowed. "Then they what?"

My mind began to race.

This is all assuming that Captain Seymour is the killer. But it could very well be anyone in town, couldn't it? And if it was anyone else in the area...

"Lily, I believe we very well may have been looking in the wrong place entirely," I said, laying a hand on her arm. "Remember that it may not have been the Captain, but someone else. It would make no sense for the poison to be from India then, would it? What if the poison was – "

" – Local," Lily said in unison with me, her eyes widening. "Sister, I believe you have a very good point."

We returned to Mrs. Lowell, asking her for information about local plants and herbs.

"Why, certainly," the woman said, rising from her seat and guiding us back toward the opposite side of the non-fiction section.

The books were decorated with paintings of plants, flowers, and insects.

"You think it might have been something concocted, not purchased?" Lily asked as we pulled every book from the shelf about the local flora.

"It has to be," I said. "I believe Doctor Webb would have recognized it otherwise. And if it came from a plant, then it is quite likely that he could have missed it entirely."

"I suppose that is possible…" Lily said.

It didn't take us long to stumble upon a variety of local plants that were characterized as "poisonous."

"Perhaps it was belladonna," Lily said, reading through a slim, ancient looking text. "*Said to cause hallucinations, loss of balance, and a rash…*"

"Doctor Webb would have noticed a rash, surely," I said. "What of foxglove? I'm certain I've seen it around. Although, it seems that it would cause a great deal of vomiting…and we didn't see any of that…"

"That likely would have been another sign for Doctor Webb," Lily said.

My eyes widened as they fell across a sketch of a rather lovely purple flower at the bottom of the page.

"Monkshood…" I murmured. "*It is said that the deadly Monkshood, or Wolfsbane, it's more commonly known name, is as dangerous as it is beautiful. Its deceiving and lovely petals hide its ability to kill a grown man within an hour of ingestion – "*

"That would explain the time after Mr. Morton left the pub," Lily said, eyes nearly bulging.

"It is preceded by problems of the digestive tract, a burning in the mouth and face, and may include sweating, dizziness, and confusion." I looked up. "These could easily be dismissed as intoxication, couldn't they?"

"Precisely what I thought," Lily said, already getting to her feet.

"There's an entire field of the stuff growing by Mrs. Bartmore's old cottage. I remember when she was alive she used to keep it in her garden, despite the fact that everyone told her how dangerous it was. 'I have no plans to eat it,' she'd say, 'I just think it's pretty to look at'," I said, my voice high in a poor imitation of the woman. "It would be incredibly simple to collect some from there."

We wasted no time in gathering our things and leaving the library, realizing there was not a great deal of sunlight left to search with.

As we traipsed up the hill, the amber setting sun at our backs, we were greeted with a vista of purple flowers, all crushed and picked, smashed into the ground, almost as far as the eye could see.

"Look here," Lily said, pointing down at the ground. "Footprints."

"They must belong to whoever did this," I said,

gesturing to the downed plants. "And whoever it was did not want these flowers to be discovered."

"I think you have very nearly solved this case, sister," Lily said. "Well done."

"Not yet," I said. "There is still one place left to look. And I believe it will answer the question of who killed Mr. Morton."

15

Lily did not think my plan was as brilliant as I did.

"Why didn't we do this sooner?" she asked. "It might have saved us a great deal of headache."

"And gone on what information?" I asked as we hurried back through town. "We would have gone in without any sort of direction. But now we have a clue. A rather large clue, if you ask me."

The lamplighter had already been through, and all the streetlights were glowing brightly. A welcome sight, since the sun had set nearly a quarter of an hour ago.

"Mr. Andrews would have shared what information he knew with Constable Brown, surely," Lily said, her hands knotting in the fabric of her skirts as she tried to keep her hem from dragging along the dirty street.

"Perhaps the Constable wouldn't have known what questions to ask, exactly," I said. "What we know now is that the Monkshood must have been used. Why would someone have gone and destroyed it otherwise?"

The windows from the pub glowed brightly, with shadows moving within indicating a great many visitors.

"I am not certain this is wise," Lily remarked, frowning. "A pub is hardly a suitable establishment for two ladies of our standing, especially unaccompanied. Remember that we are business owners and have our reputations to consider. What will people say?"

"I'm quite aware it may be viewed as an impropriety, thank you," I said.

"We will be attracting the wrong sort of attention. If word travels around, what will our clientele think?" she asked.

"We have little choice," I said. "This is a desperate situation, which calls for a degree of risk…"

We stepped in through the doorway, and a shiver ran down my spine despite the roasting heat that greeted me.

The air smelled of charred meats and onions, as well as stale wine. The smoke from the fires and from the pipes clamped between the teeth of old farmers clung to the ceiling like the clouds of a rainstorm.

Pulling my handkerchief out, I pressed it to my face as I braved the interior.

Worn tables with dents and scrapes were scattered around the room, many of which were filled with people sitting in chairs around them.

I recognized most of the patrons, the husbands and brothers and sons of our shop customers here in town. I noticed Mr. Sawyer and his son playing cards, and Mr. Newman sitting with Mr. Hobbs. Mr. Newman waved kindly at Lily and me, although his expression betrayed his surprise at our entrance.

"What are the pair of you doing around here?" asked Mr. Clark. I hadn't seen him until he had stepped up to us in the haze.

"Oh, Mr. Clark," I said. "We are here to see the proprietor, Mr. Andrews. Where might we find him?"

"What might you need him for?" Mr. Clark asked.

"Why we are here is our own business, Mr. Clark," Lily said in a cool manner. "But I must admit that it is rather urgent. So if you will please excuse us, we have a great deal to be getting on with."

She gave me a rather forceful shove further into the pub.

"That was rude," I muttered to her.

"Yes, well, I do not want to be here any longer than we must," Lily said. "Just look at the stares we are receiving."

She was not wrong.

The counter at the back of the room was filled with more people seated on the stools in front of it. Most had a tankard in hand or one sitting on the bar top in front of them.

Mr. Andrews, however, stood behind the counter with a crisp, white apron tied around his waist. His bottlebrush moustache, as dark as night and impressive as ever, twitched as he looked up and found us standing at the counter.

In his surprise, he nearly dropped the tankard in his hands. "Good evening to you, ladies. What, uh – what can I do for you?"

"We are sorry to disturb you on such a busy night," I said with as sweet a smile as I could muster. "But we have some important questions to ask you, Mr. Andrews, if you wouldn't mind obliging?"

"Questions?" he asked, setting the tankard down, his eyebrows, like caterpillars, scurrying across his face to form one line. "What sort of questions?"

"Simple questions, Mr. Andrews," Lily said, the impatience clear in her voice. "It won't take but a moment."

Mr. Andrews glanced between us, and then down the bar at a younger gentleman standing behind the counter, chatting with some of the patrons.

"Scotty, watch the counter," Mr. Andrews said, giving both Lily and me a somewhat skeptical look. "It seems I need to step away for a moment."

The man called Scotty nodded in reply, and Mr. Andrews walked along to the far end of the counter, where he lifted the thin, hinged hatch and ducked beneath it.

"Follow me, then," he said, waving us down toward a hall at the back of the room.

Lily gave me a look of warning, but followed after him.

He led us to what appeared to be an office, with a

pair of desks, shelves stacked in such an unorganized manner that I was certain they would fall at any moment, and the heavy stench of tobacco permeating every surface.

"Eh...go ahead and have a seat," Mr. Andrews said, brushing some loose papers from a pair of chairs along the wall.

"That's perfectly all right, Mr. Andrews, I think I would prefer to stand," Lily said.

And then she turned and nodded at me.

Oh, I am to be the one to ask these questions?...Very well...

Mr. Andrews looked back and forth between us. From this distance, I could make out the beads of sweat clinging to his forehead; the main room in the pub had been quite warm. "My apologies, ladies, but I do not have the liberty of extensive free time," he said. "What is it that you need?"

I cleared my throat. *How can I best approach this?*

"Mr. Andrews, we were wondering if you remembered anything strange occurring the night that Mr. Morton died," I said. I was pleasantly surprised at how even my voice was.

His eyes narrowed, his brow knitting together in several lines of wrinkles. "Begging your pardon, but what does that terrible business have to do with either of you?" he asked. "You ladies mustn't trouble yourselves with such an unpleasant matter."

"Are we not allowed to ask questions as concerned citizens?" Lily asked, jumping in for me.

Mr. Andrews frowned uncertainly. "I suppose…" he said. "But your questions might be better asked of Constable Brown."

"We have already spoken with him," Lily said. "And he refused to tell us any more than what we already know. But doesn't it trouble you, Mr. Andrews, that the last place where the unfortunate Mr. Morton happened to be alive was in your pub?"

Color rose in Mr. Andrews cheeks, while my heart began to race. *Lily, what are you doing? You're only going to make him angry.*

"Are you suggesting I had something to do with his death?" Mr. Andrews asked. "That is a very bold accusation, Miss Dickinson. I would tread carefully if I were you…"

"I am most certainly not making any accusation," Lily said, her own expression darkening. "If anything, we were just as likely as you to have been involved, given our proximity to the place of his death."

"Please, Mr. Andrews…" I said. "The sooner the authorities are able to locate the killer, the sooner we can all ensure our reputations remain intact."

His gaze shifted slowly back and forth between us. "I have a great deal of respect for you ladies," he said slowly, as if choosing his words carefully. "And I do not believe you would bring these questions to me unless you were truly worried."

"Yes, exactly," I said. It wasn't entirely untrue. We were worried. "The idea of someone walking around this town having murdered Mr. Morton…it's almost too much to bear."

"How do you think I feel, knowing the poor fool was sitting here in my pub that night?" he asked, planting his hands on his hips. He exhaled, his cheeks puffing out. "I am sorry, but as I told Constable Brown, nothing went on that night that gave me reason to suspect anything."

"What about all the patrons who stopped in that evening before Mr. Morton's demise?" Lily asked. "I assume you gave a list to the Constable?"

"Indeed I did, but there must have been fifty people here that night. It is always possible that my memory is faulty, and I forgot a few faces…and if I did, it is possible that one of those faces was the one the Constable would be looking for in the first place."

"I see," I said. "And what of those sitting with Mr. Morton? Could you remember anything about them?"

"I remember Morton as well as I might anyone else that night. I realize it's frustrating that I don't recall anything. But why would I have had any reason to pay that table special attention? It wasn't as if I knew anything was to happen."

Lily let out a heavy sigh. "Very well," she said. "I certainly hope the authorities can sort this all out soon. I, for one, am becoming rather tired of hearing everyone speak of nothing else."

"Agreed," Mr. Andrews said. "It seems to be all my customers wish to talk about." Well…may I walk you ladies out?"

We knew there was nothing else to be gleaned from this interaction, and so we allowed him to walk with us from his office back to the main room of the pub.

It was so much warmer than it was in his office, and it seemed that some newer faces had arrived.

"Thank you for your cooperation, Mr. Andrews," Lily said.

"Yes, thank you," I said.

He nodded. "I hope the same as you do, that this whole matter is soon resolved. I should very much like to have my business's good reputation back, and not frighten anyone away with thoughts that they might drop dead at any moment in my pub."

"I imagine all will come out right, eventually," I said.

He inclined his head once more and turned to move back toward the bar.

As Lily and I turned toward the door, Lily's voice dropped.

"Isn't that Doctor Webb's assistant?" she asked, pointing to a young man sitting by himself off in the corner. "I wonder why he is here all alone."

My eyes fell upon him, and I wondered if he often came here to keep his own company. *Why would he do that? He must be rather lonely. Or perhaps he is simply caught up in his thoughts.*

"I wonder if he was here the night Mr. Morton was killed," I said. "And I wonder if he saw anything – "

A sudden thought struck me.

"Lily, do you remember what Doctor Webb said about William?" I asked. "About how bright he was? And what he was so well versed in?"

"Yes," Lily answered. "He said he was '*well versed in natural forms of medicine.*' If I recall correctly."

"Lily..." I breathed, caught up in this new idea. "You don't think...?"

I turned to meet her expression, and it was the same as my own.

Suspicious.

"We should go speak with him," I said.

"No," Lily said. "Absolutely not – "

I didn't wait for her disapproval. I marched between the tables, heading for the young man.

He looked up, seeing me, and his face went pale. It was as if he somehow knew the reason I was approaching him.

Before I had a chance to say anything, he leapt up from the table and bolted for the door.

16

"Did he...did he just run?" I asked.

Stunned into complete silence, I could do nothing more than stare after William as he yanked open the door to the pub and took off out into the darkening night.

"Come, Iris, we must catch up to him!" my sister said. "We must know why he is fleeing!"

It seemed her previous caution had melted away.

We rushed after him, out into the cool night air. Darkness had properly fallen since we entered the pub, with only the last few tendrils of deepest maroon clinging to the horizon in the far distance. They, too, would disappear in just a few moments.

"William, wait!" Lily cried. "We only want to speak with you!"

We both had our skirts hiked up just enough to be able to run, though William had been able to make a great deal more headway than we could, given his trousers and long legs.

He made a dash for the end of the street, and I wondered if he was heading to Doctor Webb's clinic. Why would he go there?

"He's getting away," I said. "What do we do now?"

I didn't have to wonder for long.

Up ahead, Captain Seymour stepped out of his front door just as William passed by.

He glanced at the young man running by, and then down the street at Lily and I, who were creating quite an unladylike spectacle as we tried our best to keep up with him.

Without hesitation, Captain Seymour reached out with one of his large hands, and grabbed William by the back of his coat just as he was almost out of reach.

"Let go of me!" William cried as I nearly stumbled to a stop beside the Captain.

Lily, too, slowed, though she seemed to have a great deal more composure than I did. Had she even broken a sweat?

"What the devil is going on here?" Captain Seymour demanded. "I assume they have a perfectly good reason for chasing after you?" he asked William.

William struggled against the Captain's grip but he was a great deal smaller, and had not even a fraction of his strength. "Unhand me this instant!" he said.

"No, I daresay I will not," Captain Seymour said. "Not until these good ladies tell me why it was they were chasing you."

At that, William stopped struggling, his back turned to us.

Captain Seymour raised his eyebrows. "Well? What happened?"

Lily pursed her lips. "We have reason to suspect that William knows something about the death of Mr. Morton."

"No, I don't!" William protested, swiveling around as best he could with Captain Seymour holding him firmly in place. "I – I didn't do anything!"

Captain Seymour's eyes nearly popped out of his skull. "That's a weighty claim," he said, his left brow arching menacingly. I imagined more than one young recruit had cowered beneath that stern gaze during his military days. "Why do you think he had any involvement?" he asked.

"It's simple, really," Lily said, her gaze like daggers as she glared at William. "William is Doctor Webb's assistant. And according to Doctor Webb, William is quite the expert in natural medicine."

A perplexed expression appeared on the Captain's face. "I do not quite understand."

"Mr. Morton was killed by poisoning," I said. "And we believe it was done by means of a local flower, not some complicated or foreign concoction."

The Captain's expression softened slightly. *Did he hear the rumors, then, that it was he who killed Mr. Morton?*

"A tincture made from Monkshood, likely," Lily said. "And with William's expertise in natural medicines, flowers and herbs would certainly fall under that. I imagine the idea would have been very easy for him to form, as he already had knowledge of which poisonous flower to use so that it would be difficult to detect, even by a doctor."

Captain Seymour gave William a rough shake.

William's body rattled like a ragdoll.

"Well?" the Captain asked. "What say you? Does this claim have any merit? Huh? Answer me!"

It might have been easy to believe that William had lost consciousness, for he refused to speak, or even to move, for a few moments.

"It was – it was an accident!" William cried suddenly, covering his face with his hands. "I was trying to help him. But I was too late…"

"Help him?" I asked.

"You really expect us to believe that?" Lily asked, folding her arms. "Ridiculous."

"No," William pleaded, his eyes glassy and wide. "I am telling the truth! The tankard – it was – was never meant for Mr. Morton. His death was an accident!"

My heart sank. "An accident?" I asked. "How?"

"You'd best explain yourself…" Captain Seymour said in a voice so low that it might have been mistaken for a growl. "And you'd best do it quick, lest I take to beating the truth out of you before dragging you down to Constable Brown's."

William shuddered, leaning as far away from the Captain as he could.

"How was it an accident?" Lily asked. "Because this sounds like nothing more than an excuse to me."

"It's not an excuse," William said, desperation coating his every word. "I – I promise you!"

"Then where did the poison come from?" I asked. "Why was it even there? Was it yours? And what's this about a tankard? I thought Mr. Morton was poisoned by needle?"

William's face paled. His shoulders sagged, and he looked away. "…I will explain everything," he said, his tone defeated. "The poison was mine. But as I said, it was never meant for Mr. Morton."

"Then who *was* it meant for?" Captain Seymour asked.

William flinched, wringing his hands together. "For – for Sam Franklin," he said. With that admission, his entire demeanor changed. Regret, clear on his face, made the muscles in his neck tense, his jaw clench, and his brow tighten.

"Sam Franklin?" Captain Seymour asked, turning his face toward Lily and me.

"A very accomplished and agreeable young man in town," Lily explained.

Quite high praise from my sister.

"Why would you want to kill him?" I asked. "What was the reason for this madness?"

William looked up at me, sheepish. "I thought that might be obvious," he said. "I thought everyone in town knew that I was courting Melody Wringler."

The Captain shook his head. "I assume this Mr. Franklin had started to come between you two?" he asked.

William swallowed hard, nodding. "It happened without my knowledge," he said. "I thought everything was perfectly fine with Melody and I. We were to be married in the spring. I had proposed this past August, and I thought she was as happy as any girl should be when asked for her hand in marriage."

"Apparently she was not," Lily said.

"No...it seems she had decided that her prospects were better elsewhere," William said, an edge to his words as he stared darkly at the ground.

"So she jilted you," Captain Seymour said. "Is that any reason to try and kill the other man involved?"

William's eyes, suddenly taking on a slightly crazed look, bulged as he looked up at the Captain. "If he was out of the way, then there would be no reason for Melody not to choose me," he said. "She would see that she was wrong all along, and that she should have remained loyal to me as I have to her – "

"This has gone far beyond jealousy and rage," Captain Seymour said, his expression like that of a judge pronouncing a final sentence. "To go so far as to try and kill a man...it's despicable."

William hung his head, and it took a great deal of effort for me not to pity him.

There was still the matter of Mr. Morton, however. An innocent man caught in a lover's quarrel.

"But what you are saying is this had absolutely nothing to do with Mr. Morton," I said. "How was it that he came to consume this poison meant for Mr. Franklin?"

William's jaw, tightly clenched, loosened enough for him to open it briefly and speak again. "I was to meet Mr. Franklin at the pub that night, though I have since learned that he had no intention of honoring my invitation. I had decided to poison his drink, which I had ordered for him beforehand. I had hoped he would drink it, hear my blessing for his relationship with Melody, and then go on home. I imagined he would be found, and it would be presumed that he suffered a heart failure or something of the sort and died."

My stomach twisted into knots. "How cruel…" I said.

"Well, it didn't happen that way. Mr. Morton sat down beside me that night, looking rather glum, already quite drunk…" William said. "He – well, he asked if the drink meant for Mr. Franklin was mine, to which I said no, and before I could stop him, he had brought it to his lips and drank half of it before I could inform him that it was for someone else."

Captain Seymour's face turned red and blotchy. "You mean to say that this all could have been prevented if you had spoken up?" he asked, tightening his hold on the back of William's coat.

William cowered beneath the Captain's height.

"But what of the puncture mark on the dead man?" I interrupted, still nagged by the thought. "Where did the needle come into it?

"I – I tried to help him," William said. "I suppose part of me, deep down, feared what I was planning to do, and so just in case something went terribly wrong or I changed my mind, I had brought a syringe filled with an antidote. I went out after Mr. Morton left the pub as inconspicuously as I could. Hardly anyone paid attention to someone as drunk as he was…I managed to catch up to him in the darkness, and tried to administer the antidote…but I was…I was too late."

My stomach dropped, and a wave of nausea washed over me. This entire tragedy could have been prevented…

Lily's face was quite reserved after his admission. For once, she was lost for words.

Captain Seymour, however, knew exactly what was to be done next.

"Come with me to the Constable," he said firmly, still grasping the back of William's jacket.

William did not obey. In one sudden motion, he managed to slide his arms out of the sleeves, untangling himself from the Captain's grip.

He spun around, something bright glinting in his right hand, flashing in the light of the streetlamps.

"No," William said, his chest heaving, his eyes as round and reflective as the moon overhead. "No, I don't think I will…"

"What did you say?" Captain Seymour growled, taking a step toward him, reaching out for him.

William stepped out, away from his grip.

The knife flashed in his hand, and I heard the sickening sound of its blade slashing through fabric…

17

"Captain!" Lily and I exclaimed in unison.

It had all happened so quickly. One moment, the Captain had had a firm grip on William's coat; it seemed there was no way for him to wrestle free.

The next, William had somehow managed to untangle himself and to pull a knife from the inside of one of his boots.

As the Captain had reached out to grab him, William's knife had sliced through the sleeve of Captain Seymour's jacket, and cut all the way down though the flesh.

I moved toward the injured man, wanting to somehow help, but Captain Seymour held one hand up, while his other, wounded arm hung limply at his side.

"No!" he warned me. "Stay back!"

"You cannot protect everyone, Captain," William

said. "I have every intention of killing all three of you. It is the only way to hide my crime."

The Captain immediately stepped between the murderer and Lily and I, clutching his wounded arm with his other hand, attempting to staunch the bleeding. "You will not lay a hand on the ladies, you scoundrel – "

"I have little care for anyone apart from myself at this point," William said harshly, holding his knife out in front of him, clutching it with both hands. Even in the darkness, it was easy to see that he was trembling. "Don't you understand? My life is ruined!"

"It was ruined the moment you chose a course of deceit and death," Lily said.

"No," William said, pointing the knife at Lily, and then back at the Captain. "No, everything was going to work out just as I wanted. Sam would have died at home. Melody would have mourned him, but I would have been there for her, been her source of comfort while she weathered the storm in her heart. And then we would have been married in the spring, just as we were meant to be!"

His voice had risen to a shout now.

Surely he will have attracted attention – someone, anyone...please, help us!

The Captain slipped his good hand behind his back, his gaze still fixed on William. "What do you want?" he asked coolly.

As he spoke, his hand balled into a fist, apart from

his pointer finger, which he jabbed repeatedly toward the door to his home.

I realized he was signaling for Lily and me to escape to safety, but my feet seemed rooted to the spot.

"Surely there must be something you want, something in place of our lives. A vow of secrecy perhaps – "

"Nothing any of you say or do will convince me of your silence," William snapped.

"I doubt that is true," Captain Seymour reasoned in a calming tone. "I am sure we can come to an agreement – "

Once again, the Captain pointed toward his home.

I glanced over at Lily, whose eyes were fixed on the Captain's back, on his hand.

When she felt my gaze on her, she locked eyes with me...and then nodded.

I willed my feet to finally move.

Almost as if of one mind, Lily and I took off at a run toward the door to Captain Seymour's house.

William saw us, and while I could not make out what words he said, as they came out in a strangled yelp of anger and fear, I knew that he would not take the action lightly.

Lily threw herself against the door at the same time that footsteps pounded against the cobblestone road behind us.

Fear shot through me, sharp and painful, as I urged Lily to pull the door open. "Come, Lily, we do not have time!"

She gripped the door handle with her shaking

hand, and yanked it outward. She dashed inside, and I was close behind her.

"Come back!" William cried, a demand that would have been comical had the circumstances been less deadly. "Come back or I'll – "

But what he was going to do, I would never know, for his words were stolen from him as he smashed into the ground just outside the front door.

I whirled to a halt, turning to see what had happened.

Captain Seymour, stretched across the ground, gripped William's leg.

"Run!" Captain Seymour yelled at us.

Lily grabbed my arm and dragged me further into the house.

She ducked out of the foyer as William's angry yells echoed across the marble floors, and I followed closely on her heels.

"What shall we do?" I asked, my chest heaving as Lily slammed the door of the dining room closed behind us. I realized belatedly that we ought to have slammed and locked the front door, but it was now too late. "He is utterly mad! And we've just trapped ourselves here in this house!"

"Perhaps," Lily said. "But we can better defend ourselves in here, can't we? Here, help me to drag this chair in front of the – "

The door crashed open a moment later, William throwing himself inside.

I let out a shriek, and hurried around the table, heading toward the door to the kitchen.

"No!" William cried, quickly blocking my path before sagging against the sideboard, clutching his ribs. Blood seeped between his fingers, and the knife was missing from his grasp. Had the Captain gotten it away from him?

But where was the Captain? What if the knife had found its way into his back?

William wrenched himself upright, letting out a cry of pain. He reached for a candlestick on the center of the table, one that had a pointed edge...like a dagger.

My throat began to close up. I couldn't swallow.

"I cannot promise you this won't hurt," William said, dragging the candlestick across the table, leaving a long, jagged scratch in the surface. "But you shouldn't have gotten involved. If you hadn't, then you and your sister..."

His eyes screwed up as he looked around.

"Where is your – "

A silver, mirrored vase shattered against William's skull. As his eyes rolled into the back of his head, he crumpled to the ground like a sack of flour.

I gasped, clutching at my chest, trying to draw in a full breath.

I could only stare down at his still form, gaping.

Lily suddenly appeared, standing from a hidden spot behind the table.

"Lily!" I exclaimed, staggering backward into the windows behind me. "Are you all right?"

"Of course." Lily tossed aside the remnants of the vase. She calmly brushed the shards that had fallen onto her skirts off onto the floor. "I realized that we were not going to make it out of this without a fight. I apologize for leaving you to be the bait, but it was the only way to ensure that he was distracted."

My heart still racing, I sank down onto a silk cushioned bench. "How did you know that would work?"

"I didn't," Lily said, wrinkling her nose in distaste as she took a wide step around William's still body to make her way toward me. "Thankfully, it seems that I have a talent for bashing people in the head. Perhaps it will come in handy again in the future."

Before I could point out that this was no time for jokes, there was a clamor in the front foyer, with several voices calling out.

"Miss Lily?" called one of those voices. "Miss Iris? Where are you?"

"The dining room," Lily said in return.

A moment later, Mr. Clark and Mr. Newman dashed into the dining room, faces flushed.

"Thank heavens…" Mr. Clark said, hurrying over to Lily. "Are you ladies all right?"

"Yes," I said. "All thanks to Lily."

"It was nothing," Lily said. "I did as I had to."

Mr. Newman bent down beside William, laying a finger against the side of his throat. "He's still alive. Not that he deserves as much…"

Evidently there had been witnesses to our earlier struggle outside after all.

Another figure dashed into the room.

"Oh, Captain Seymour!" I exclaimed. "You're alive!"

"Of course I am," he said. In the light of the dining room, I could clearly see the blood soaked into the sleeve of his coat where William had slashed him.

"Your arm," Lily said. "We must get it bandaged. Where might I find a clean cloth?"

"Don't bother," the Captain said. "I will have Doctor Webb look it over. I'm certain we will see him here shortly."

"I shall fetch the Constable," Mr. Clark said, hurrying from the room.

"And I will find rope or something for binding the villain," Mr. Newman said, getting to his feet. "If he wakes, he will likely try to fight. The man is clearly out of his mind. And the last thing we need is for anyone else to be injured."

He turned and looked at Lily.

"Well done, Miss Dickinson. You might very well have saved your sister's life as well as your own."

He, too, disappeared from the room.

"Are you both all right?" Captain Seymour asked. "I was terribly worried when the scoundrel ran in here."

"We are fine," Lily said, continuing to show remarkable composure. She looked at me. "Aren't we, Iris?"

"Now I am, yes," I said. "Captain, I was certain he had – that he had – "

The Captain reached into his coat, and pulled out the knife. He proceeded to toss it onto the table with a clatter. "No," he said. "He had no idea what it would be like to truly attack another man with such a weapon. I had more than enough experience to disarm him." He glanced down at William lying on the floor. "Though I certainly do not thank him for bloodying my floor…"

He looked at us.

"But I must ask…" he said. "Did you originally think it was I who poisoned Mr. Morton?"

I opened my mouth, and then closed it promptly.

"We suspected it," Lily said. "Which I regret now, as we had heard it from Mrs. Minford, and I should know better than to listen to anything she says."

"We're sorry, Captain," I said. "I am ashamed to ever have believed it."

"It's perfectly all right," he said. "I am the newest face in town, after all. Morton's death happened so soon after my arrival."

"It is unacceptable," Lily said.

"No," the Captain said. "What is unacceptable is that this man chose to do what he did, and unsettled the whole town in the process. He is to blame for all of this. Let us forgive one another and move past it. Agreed?"

"Agreed," Lily said.

"Agreed," I said.

18

I had never realized how comfortable my bed could be once a matter that caused such great tension had been resolved. After William had been arrested and confessed to his crimes, Lily and I had spent the rest of the night answering questions about what we had learned.

Constable Brown, instead of being angry with our interference as I had feared he might be, was quite impressed and very nearly overjoyed with it. He felt foolish for overlooking alternative forms of poisons, and said that he might have saved all of us a great deal of trouble.

All was well, and as dawn appeared over the edge of the gorge, we went home to rest.

The curtains drawn, Lily insisted that I get to bed as soon as I could.

"What about you?" I asked her.

"I shall make some tea," she said. "And then I shall

be ready for bed as well. I seem to have discovered a knack for doing battle with murderous villains, but even I need a little time to settle down after such madness."

I wished to stay awake with her, but I could hardly keep my eyes open.

"Very well," I said. "I shall see you in a few hours."

"Yes," Lily said. "Rest well."

I sank into the sheets, cool and soft, a few moments later, and fell into a deep, sound sleep.

A LOUD *CRASH* caused me to sit straight up.

I blinked a few times, my mind fuzzy, my mouth dry.

I looked around. The sun had changed. It must have been late afternoon or evening.

Lily's bed, still empty on the other side of the room, sent a shiver of panic through me.

"Lily?" I spoke into the stillness.

The house was quiet, and it took me a long, hard moment to realize that the crash I'd heard had not been in this room at all, but in a bad dream.

As I thought of it, I realized that the dream I'd had felt...familiar, somehow.

I couldn't remember it well. Shadows pressed in on all corners of my mind, and it was as if I had been staring through a foggy window.

I couldn't recall anything I had seen, and already

the remnants of fear dwindled. My palms, slick with sweat, were beginning to dry. My heart, beating rapidly, was beginning to slow.

What was I so afraid of?

It was a different kind of fear than what I had felt when William chased us. That had been potent, certainly…but this dread was deep, like an unhealed wound.

"Lily?" I asked.

For some reason, this nightmare felt like more than a simple dream. It was as if recent events had shaken loose something in the back of my mind…perhaps a memory long since forgotten.

But what might have happened to me that would cause me to feel such great fear?

I hurried to the door into the sitting room, and pulled it open. "Lily – "

"Iris, what is it?"

I found Lily sitting in a chair beside the fireplace, lowering a book down into her lap. A fresh cup of tea sat beside her on the side table.

"Oh, thank heavens…" I said, going to her. "I just had a terrible dream, and heard this awful crash, and worried that something had happened – "

"It was just a nightmare," Lily said, reaching out and laying her hand on my arm. "It is perfectly understandable after what we have just experienced."

"No," I said, shaking my head, cold sweat clinging to my forehead. "No, this was different. I have had this dream before, but I am not even sure it *was* a dream – "

"Iris," Lily said more firmly, squeezing my arm slightly. "You must calm yourself. You are sounding hysteric."

"But why do I feel so frightened?" I asked. "It's as if…as if I am trying to remember something that happened a long time ago, something terrible – something dreadful – "

Lily stood from her seat, and wrapped her arm around my shoulder. "There now, sister…" she said. "Whatever it is you think you remember, you are mistaken."

"But – " I said.

"Iris," Lily said more harshly. "That is enough of this. Some things are best left alone."

My eyes widened. *So I was correct…she knows something about the thing I am starting to remember.*

Lily guided me back to the bedroom, where she urged me to get back into bed. She brought me a hot cup of tea, and treated me as if I had fallen ill. She spoke kindly to me, but there was a distance in her eyes, and I became aware that she averted her gaze whenever she came near me.

What is it that she does not wish to discuss? What happened in my past that my mind found too terrible to remember, and that Lily is too frightened to speak of?

I decided not to keep asking, as it was clear I would get no answers and it would only distress her once again.

She left me alone just as the sun had set, ending another day and bathing the town outside in a warm, golden glow. Yet, somehow, my heart would not feel any warmth.

I shall not bring up this memory again tonight. But that does not mean I will let it rest forever.

If the recent events had taught me anything, it was that dark secrets would always come to light...

One day, I would address the matter with my sister again. Until then, I would ponder the mystery. Perhaps thinking of it more would draw it closer to the surface.

Fear bubbled inside me.

Is it something I will want to remember? Will I regret it once I do?

There was only one way to find out.

Continue following the mysterious adventures of the Dickinson sisters in "A Pattern of Death."

EXCERPT

From "A Pattern of Death: The Dickinson Sisters Mysteries, Book 2."

There were no words that could be said about the situation in which we found ourselves. Nothing could have prepared us for the horror that greeted us, as silently as the grave itself.

I couldn't help myself. I followed after Constable Brown as he made his way toward the chair. Everything within me screamed at me to stop, to stay away, to save myself the countless sleepless nights and the haunting thoughts that were sure to follow after me.

But I couldn't stop my footsteps. I took a step toward the chair. Then another. I could see the puddle beneath the chair was red. It had run through the cracks in the wooden floor. It would likely never fully come out.

I took another step. Level with the chair, I could see

the top of the victim's head. He might have been sleeping. Or perhaps staring absentmindedly into the fire.

Another step. The way he was slumped over made my stomach twist in knots.

Don't look. You will regret it for the rest of your life if you do.

I blinked, my heartbeat slowing...very nearly coming to a halt.

Stay away! Your imagination will suffice! You need not scar yourself!

My pulse thundered in my ears.

A knife. The glassy, vacant expression in his eyes. The blood...

Transfixed, I stood there, staring. Gaping. Unable to look away. Glued to the spot. My knees locked. My breath caught in my throat. My head pounded.

I didn't know if the screams were in my mind or out loud, but either way, they sent chills through my bones.

"Miss Dickinson..."

A voice attempted to draw my attention, to make me turn my head.

The knife must have struck its victim in the heart. He didn't look as if he had the chance to get up. Whatever had happened, whoever had done this, hadn't even given him a chance.

His shirt must have been green at one point, for the sleeves seemed to be a deep olive color, but the chest, from his shoulders down...scarlet.

The blade itself was intricate in design. Not a

simple kitchen knife or a letter opener. The grip, wrapped in leather, looked expertly crafted, and the metal itself gleamed like moonlight on a still pond.

"Miss Dickinson, come with me."

My body was physically shifted away, turned from the corpse. My eyes might have been staring at the dining table, my feet carrying me away from the blood, from the smell – but that didn't mean that I could see anything apart from the dead body, seated in the large chair as if enjoying a late morning rest.

"Get her something to drink. Something cold."

Whose voice was that?

I found myself sitting. I blinked, my cheeks wet.

"Miss, you must breathe."

Breathing. Yes. That was important, wasn't it? In order to ensure that I, myself, did not end up a corpse.

END OF EXCERPT

ABOUT THE AUTHOR

Blythe Baker is the lead writer behind several popular historical and paranormal mystery series. When Blythe isn't buried under clues, suspects, and motives, she's acting as chauffeur to her children and head groomer to her household of beloved pets. She enjoys walking her dog, lounging in her backyard hammock, and fiddling with graphic design. She also likes binge-watching mystery shows on TV.

To learn more about Blythe, visit her website and sign up for her newsletter at www.blythebaker.com

Made in the USA
Columbia, SC
19 April 2022